HELL HAS NO FURY 2:
Eye For an Eye

HELL HAS NO FURY 2:
Eye For an Eye

By

J.J. Jackson

Felony Books, a division of Olive Group, LLC,
P.O. Box 1577, Belton, MO 64012

This book is a work of fiction. Names, characters, places, and incidents are products of the author's imagination or are used fictitiously. Any resemblance to actual events or locales or persons living or dead is entirely coincidental.

ISBN-13: 978-1974466627

Felony Books 1st edition September 2017

10 9 8 7 6 5 4 3 2 1

Manufactured in the United States of America

For information regarding special discounts for bulk purchases, please contact Felony Books at felonybooks@gmail.com.

Books by J.J. Jackson:

O.P.P.
O.P.P. 2
O.P.P. 3
A CLASSY THUG
REVENGE IS BEST SERVED COLD
REVENGE IS BEST SERVED COLD 2
SCANDALS OF A CHI-TOWN THUG
HELL HAS NO FURY
21 DAYS OF SECRETS

www.felonybooks.com

Chapter 1

Shawn sits at the kitchen window looking at the rain falling from the sky. Every day he watches the kids in the neighborhood playing. People going to work, coming home. He wonders why no one is noticing him.

Blair has been MIA for 30 days. She's off with Kurt living her life. She purchased a home in the Dominican Republic and Costa Rica with her husband's money. Now you know she didn't leave her mother out. They're like a package deal. She purchased her mother a nice six bedroom house in Brunswick Island, North Carolina. Her mother loves it there. She lives right on the beach, her sons in tow.

Although she's still in school, Blair purchased Rena a fully furnished house in Woodmere development. Blair lied, telling Rena that Shawn filed for divorce, leaving her with two million in alimony. Rena bought it. It's easy to believe because Blair only stayed in their Fort Washington house wit Shawn for six months. One day she was reading a *Honeymoon* magazine and a picture of Costa Rica caught her eye. She had to go. She called Kurt, told him her plan, he was all in. One week later they were off. They stayed in the Sandal Resort, met another couple. Sandy and Clint, they been married just 3 days. The two set of couples hit it off right away, so much in common. Blair law school, Sandy a lawyer. Kurt used to be a dope boy, Clint a drug counselor. Their conversations were endless. Blair, along with Kurt, acted as if they were married. Kurt knows he veered from the street rulebook putting him in violation, but he doesn't care. He's riding the white horse; it's feeling damn good right about now.

Blair doesn't even think about Shawn. She's hoping he dies from starvation. She told herself no one will even know he's in the house anyway. No one can get in. All the doors are locked. His doctor's office called her, she told them she has another doctor for him. They never called again. Blair is happy, looking the part as she hangs on to Kurt.

Kurt is bald headed, still keeping his facial hair. He keeps it trim, close cut lining his narrow brown skinned face. His nose is sharp, lips small, eyes grey. He stands 6 feet 6 inches solid. His body ... cut the fuck up. This places him in category 10 on the man scale, which makes him a Casanova—the highest looks of all.

Chapter 2

Back in Maryland, Shawn sits in his normal spot unable to move. He catches sight of this stranger coming up his driveway with papers in hand.

Ding Ding! The doorbell rings. Of course it's nothing he can do about it. *Ding, Ding, Ding, Ding!* She rings again and again.

He's so frustrated that he can't move his wheel chair to get the door.

"I know someone is sitting in the window. I saw him. I wonder if he's deaf?" she says out loud to herself. Shuffling her feet over to the window, she stands in front of Shawn's view. "Hello," she mouths.

Shawn blinks fast, hoping she'll get the message to help him. He's so weak. It's good he can still blink his eyes.

She notices he's blinking. Walking across the street she knocks on his neighbor's door.

The man opens his door. "May I help you?"

"Yes, I was wondering about that man sitting in the window over there …" She points to Shawn. "Is he sick?"

"Not sure. He sits there all the time."

"So you know him?" she asks.

"Not really. I use to see him at times, coming and going but now he just sits like he's waiting on someone to come by or something."

"You never became curious about that?" It don't strike you as odd?" she appeals.

"Now really, ma'am, I mind my business. I was brought up that way, you know."

"Thanks, sir. Sorry for taking up your time."

"Sorry I couldn't be of more help to you."

She makes her way back to Shawn's house, standing in front of him again. He's blinking fast. All of a sudden tears flood his face. She covers her heart with her free hand.

"Oh my God, something's not right. I knew it." Running to her car she dials 911.

"Hello, what's your emergency?"

Chapter 3

"Kurt, I'm just loving this day. The breeze feels so good. The music. Maybe we should buy a home here too," Blair voices as the two of them sit along the Riviera dining at the Punta Monterrey Beach Hotel in Punta Mita Resort.

He gleams. "Blair, we can't be buying up everything. We don't work nowhere. We gotta start making plans, like investments."

With her elbow on the table she folds one hand under her chin. "What type you have in mind?"

"Stock. Flipping houses. Shit like dat. We got 6 houses. We've traveled all over, week after week. Now it's time for making bread, feel me?"

"How about you take care of that department and I keep taking care of you."

Giving her a sardonic grin, "Whatever you say."

"Good. Can we order now, 'cause I want dessert," she tells him.

"Do the damn thang," he comments, thinking, *She's nice but so fuckin green. You never trust nobody wit yo ends. I'ma have it all soon. Baltimore here I come, back on top real soon. All I gotta do is keep slinging this dick, keep her fed. She's already hooked!*

Chapter 4

"Wait, maybe he don't want the police in his business. I know I wouldn't. Not if it wasn't a life threatening situation."

She presses the end button on her cell, puts down her Jehovah witness papers, slams her car door shut, pitter patters her way back to Shawn's house, standing in front of his window once again.

"If you understand me, blink one time," she orders.

He blinks one time. "Good," she pronounces slowly.

"Do you want me to call the police?"

He blinks two times.

"I guess that means no?"

He blinks once, acknowledging that means no.

"Ok," she pronounces slowly again.

"Lady, that man is retarded!" a boy on his bike yells as he passes by.

Paying his little bad ass no mind, she looks around unsure as to how she'll get in the house. "Awe." A thought remotely pops into her head. Holding up one finger at him, she then jogs around the back of the house. *Good, a glass patio door.* Scanning the backyard she lays eyes on a baseball bat that's laying in the middle of the yard.

"That's what I need." She runs over, picks it up and runs back to the door. She swings.

Wham!

Shawn hears the glass break. He's so ecstatic. Taking precaution she opens the door, not knowing if there's a dog or someone else in the house. She moves about looking for Shawn. Standing in the kitchen door way, "My God, what's that smell?!" She covers her nose with her forearm. The odor gets stronger the closer she gets to Shawn. Laying hands on the handles of his wheel chair, she turns him facing her.

Involuntary she flinches. "My God what happened to you? Who left you here like this?" She asks these questions because Shawn looks like a dying mouse. His face is sunken, eyes popping out his very dry cracking skin. His facial hair, along with the hair on his head, is matted. He hasn't eaten in almost two months. No water in 30 days, since the last drop Blair made while visiting Rena.

Immediately she opens the refrigerator. Nothing. She eyeballs an empty glass, fills it with tap water, racing to Shawn holding it to his mouth.

"I know it's tap water; it won't hurt you. Please drink it."

That he does. It's so good to him.

When he's done, "You want more?"

He blinks one time. She fills the glass back up. This time she grabs the kitchen towel. He spilled so much on himself the first time trying to drink so fast.

After the third fill up, "We need to get you cleaned you up," she yaks.

Shawn's so happy to see his knight and shining angel. He doesn't even care if she sees him naked. His butt's so sore from sitting in shit and piss. That warm bath is music to his ears.

She wheels him off to the bathroom. "Thank God you have a full bath on this floor. I was uncertain how I was going to make those long steps with you in hand." She runs this bath water. "Now you're going to have to work with me."

She pulls him up by his under arms. Shawn can't feel a thing. She peels his clothes off. His ass is full of shit, piss and blood.

"*Whoo,* boy you smell," she says, frowning up her nose.

"I'm gonna have to push you in, ok?"

He blinks once.

Then it dawns on her he's paralyzed from the neck down. So she pushes him in. Water splashes on both of them. She stumbles forward.

"*Whoo*, I almost was taking a bath with you."

She watches him for a few minutes, then she runs more hot water in the tub.

"It's time to bathe you. My name is Mrs. Scott. I'm a Physical Therapist at Southern hospital. Jehovah works in mysterious ways. I usually have my partner with me but today I went out by myself just to knock on doors, handing out the watch towers."

He smiles, thinking, *I never thought I would be saved by a Jehovah witness, somebody I used to hide from.* He blinks one time. The water feels so good to him. His ass is so sore though.

"Don't worry about the sores on your behind. I'm going to put some cream on it to make it feel better. It should help them go away. We gon' get you better, you'll see. You poor boy," she affirms, washing his back.

Chapter 5

"Kurt, I'ma lace your account wit $300,000. Can you flip it into $600,000? Then we'll have enough money to take care of us if we need it, right?" Blair lays the law down as they lay in bed.

"That'll work. I'll start making some calls. I'll start wit' flipping houses back home—"

Blair jumps up, cutting his words short. "Back home? You can't leave me. What I'ma do? Where I'ma go?"

"Slow yo roll. You going wit' me, that's what you gon' do. Let me be the man for once."

"Kurt, you are the man when you laying down that long fat pipeline. It tells me you the man."

"Come 'mere, girl." He pulls her into his arms.

Blair takes hold of his 11 inches. She pulls on it back and forth. Kurt closes his eyes, enjoying the strokes. She lay hands on the KY gel, squirts some in her hand, rubs his dick with it. Once it's evenly spread, she climbs on top, easing it in her wet pussy inch by muthafuckin inch.

She moans, "Ummm ... hmm."

Kurt takes hold of her waist, stroking her pussy like butter, making calculated moves, piercing her walls, her soft meat.

"Ummm … uh-umm, Kurt," she hisses.

Swiftly his dick moves in, out, up, around. She purrs as her wetness splashes all over his dick. Shifting gears, he flips her little ass over onto her back, lifting her legs, putting her feet together, holding on to her, he thrusts like he's a washing machine on spin cycle. He goes to work.

"Kurt! Kurt! Fuck! *Iiiii*—shit, it's too much. Fuck!"

Her whining falls on deaf ears. He's pushing up in that pussy, *Bang bang bang!* She tries to break loose. He's too strong. Taking one hand he scoops her ass up, holding one ass cheek turning her on her side. He grins, drawing back, *Bang!* Tapping that pussy, he continues to blow that pink pussy up. Her pussy creams.

"I can't take no more, baby. Cum please nut please!"

His mind isn't on her. It's on Simone, his baby momma. He can't stop as he thinks of how good her pussy is and how much he misses it. Kurt has always been long winded. Simone is the only woman that can hang with him. This is the first time he's fucked her unmercifully like this. He keeps fucking. She keeps squirting cum over and over. He loves it.

"Damn baby damn!"

He dips in and out at rapid speeds.

"Oh God." She's crying. She's loving him more and more with every stroke. "I love you, Kurt. Please don't ever leave me. I love you so much!"

She holds on to the bed post, as he takes a handful of her hair, pulling, making her feel like her neck is about to snap. He leans in, biting her leg hard as hell. She likes it like that. It makes her orgasms quick, back to back. She purrs. Her hot juices run all over him. After one hour, he pulls out, stroking his meat.

"Suck it suck it," he demands.

She gets on all fours, sucking-sucking.

"Ahhhh fuck!" he yells, busting nut all in her mouth, so much she can't swallow. He beats his dick on her face so the rest can come out. Then he flops on his back. She rolls on top of him, still crying,

"You ok, shawdy?" he yawps, rubbing her hair.

"I'm good. That was so good. Where that come from?"

He smiles, envisioning fucking Simone.

"I love you, that's all," he lies, closing his eyes thinking of Simone.

Blair's blood pumps fast towards her brain. She loves him more than she loves her own life. She'll do anything to please her boo.

Chapter 6

"What up, babe? It's me."

"You ... Where you been, Kurt? You ain't send no money. Shit, you act like I had your son alone—"

"I know. I'ma send you some money tomorrow. Postal money order, like 10G's," Kurt tells the love of his life.

"Where you at? Why you whispering?" she asks.

"I'll tell you another day. Don't give my cookie away either. I'm out here makin' moves for us. I love you. Keep my shit tight, you heard."

"Boy, I'm not thinking 'bout nobody but yo' ass," Simone expresses.

"That's right. I'on wanna hav'ta go to jail for yo ass." He sounds like he's joking but she knows all too well his get down.

"Whateva. You wanna talk to Jr.?" She references their 6-year-old son.

"Nah, I gotta get back. Kiss'em fo' a nigga dough. I gotta dip. I'ma try and hit you up tomorrow," he whispers, standing in the bathroom of Blair's house located in Costa Rica.

"Whateva you doing be careful. I want you with us in one piece like you left. Health at that!"

She knows he's with a woman. She don't care as long as she gets hers. She loves his dirty draws.

"No doubt." He throws her a kiss, ending the call.

Opening the door to the bathroom, "Who—"

"Whoo shit!" He jumps.

"You scared the shit outta me, shawdy."

"That means you ain't living right. What you doing, creepin'?" she asks him.

"No, I was using the bathroom. A nigga can use his own bathroom, can't he? I called my nephew. I was talking to his mother. She was telling me he was acting up. I told her I was sending her some funds. I felt bad 'cause I told her last week I would send some and forgot. What you doing creepin' up on me anyway?"

"I wasn't. I was going to the bathroom and here you are. You could've called them out here. Kurt, you be doing some crazy stuff, you know that."

"Did you send your son's mother some money too?" Now she's fishing,

"Hell no. I hate dat bitch. Don't mention her name again in my presence." He plays it off.

"Sorry, she is your child's mother. Dang, don't be so dag on salty."

"How you know 'bout'a anyway?" That's what he's really flexed about. He never told Blair about her.

"Kurt, you oughtta know by now I do my homework."

He gives her a crazy look. "Blair, you not a stalker or some shit like dat. You know them women that be on that show *Snapped*?"

"Hell to the no, but a person should always know who they fucking wit. Don't you agree?" she says, sitting on the toilet pissing.

"I can feel dat. But you gotta know I do have a life outside you, right?"

"Outside me? What's that supposed ta mean, nigga?" She's frizzed.

"That means you can go do things wit'out me. The same goes for me. Some days I'ma wanna hang wit my boys, right?"

"Oh you right. When we get to the states I'm going out wit Rena. You can do you wit yo boys. Not bitches, right?" she commands, wiping her ass.

"That's wussup. This way we won't smother one another. We'll crave each other, right?"

"You silly. I crave you no matter what. I'm craving you now." She holds one of her twins in her hand. "And these tits gon' show you how much I crave yo ass. I'm tattooing your name all over them. My ass too." She grins.

Fear pumps through his heart as he stands staring at her.

I gotta lay off her ass some. I think I'm giving her too much dick medication. As of today I'm pulling back.

Chapter 7

It's 8 p.m. Mrs. Scott sits at Shawn's dining room table, hand-feeding him some mash potatoes.

"Son, we have to put some meat on those bones of yours yet." She notices his mouth is cracked in the corners. He's kinda frowning up as he eats. It hurts a little so she lightens the mood some.

"Son, here is something for you. Why did the farmer feed his cows money?" She pauses. "Ok here it is—he wanted rich milk. Get it?" she says, laughing.

He follows, grinning.

It's working, she's thinking.

"Here's another one. What did one cool alien say to the other. Ok, ok ... you're a far out dude." She laughs. He does too. "Last one. What is the vampire's favorite drink?" His eye grow big like he knows it. "You know it, huh. Are you thinking ... A bloody Mary?"

He smiles, looking at her like don't stop.

"Ok one mo ... What do you call a cold rabbit sitting on a bunny … A hot dog on a bun."

He gives a crazy look.

"You didn't like that one, huh? My grandson by my oldest daughter tells me those jokes. Look, you ate it all up. Here." She wipes him up then coats his lips wit Blistex. Shawn feels much better.

Turning his wheelchair around, she starts wheeling him to his room. They come up to his study. She stops.

"Let's go in here to see what book I can read to you."

She wheels him in. Making a turnabout, she faces him seeing his eyes are open so wide.

"What's wrong?"

He roams his eyes towards the right. She follows, walking over towards where he's looking. She observes the area.

"Nothing over here, son."

His eyes grow bigger. She looks around, scanning his face.

"What are you trying to tell me? I tell you what. I'll roll you over here." She does so.

He sits staring at the books. She runs her hands across them when she lands on *Hush Love* by Jordan Belcher. He blinks rapidly.

"You want me to read this one to you?" She tugs on the book, trying to remove it. To her surprise the shelf slides to the side.

"Oh my!" She jumps.

Sticking her head in she sees it's a ramp. Wheeling him in within 5 seconds the shelf closes with a steel door sealing them in.

"Wow! This is beautiful," she comments, looking at all the gym equipment, 60 inch TV's, fire places, kitchen, three-bedroom, cameras, a whole 'nother house. A rambler style house at that, as if they're in a panic room. The screens on the walls show every room in the house and the outside of the house as well.

His eyes motion her to go to the big vault that sits on the floor by the fireplace. Good thing it's not locked. She opens it.

With her mouth open she turns to him, "Oh my God, son, nothing but guns. What in God's name are you into? Who are you?" She notices the painting of his mother, father and him. Automatically she covers her mouth. "Bill is your father? Your Bill's son? I used to date him in school. Well we dated for a minute. You know how that goes. He was a lady's man." Shawn smiles. "He also was—" She cuts herself off. "Anyway, he made money. Let me put it that way."

She wasn't sure if Shawn knew his father was a pimp as well as a coke dealer.

She wheels him to the biggest bedroom.

"Let's get in this big king size bed. You need some sleep. Don't worry, I'm going to take good care of you."

Shawn looks over at his dresser drawer. Mrs. Scott's getting the hang of his language. She opens the top drawer.

"Damn!" she blurts, surveying all the damn money in it.

His eyes go up and down, telling her to take some.

"You want me to have some?"

He blinks once.

"But for what?"

His eyes look out into the sophisticated gym equipment.

"I get it. You want me to help you get back on your feet. First I have to know what's wrong with you. I saw some hospital papers upstairs. I'll check them out, call around as well. For now get some sleep."

She helps him into the bed, takes $1,000 so she can get him some food.

"Bye now. Get some sleep. You need it, rest comfortable. I'll be back in the morning if Jehovah's willing."

Chapter 8

One Month Has Passed

"I wanna go see if his ass is dead so bad, but then again I'on want nobody to see me going in and out that house too much. On second thought I'll just play this hotel for now. Where is Rena's ass? That hoe always late. The party gon' be over by time we get there," she self communicates out loud while watching ratchet TV.

Her cell phone breaks her thoughts of her and Kurt's last sextacy. She looks at her cell. A text.

Rena: I'm in the parking lot hoe.
Blair: As always late as hell. I'm coming.

She turns the tube off, seizes her Louis V bag, then brushes her way out the door.

"Hey bitch, where you been dang?" Blair hollas, getting in Rena's 5.0.

"I had to feed Blue's ass. You know his old ass love chewing on this pussy."

"Now that's just downright nasty thinking his ass gumming on your shit makes my skin crawl, yuck. You love them old ass men. You need ta get you a man around your age or some'em," Blair informs.

"When you find one with good sense send his ass my way then," Rena states, pulling out the parking lot.

"Sorry boo, Kurt's taken," Blair remarks.

"Kurt ain't my type any ole way. I like them Biggy Small type nuccas, trust that. I'ing into them pretty boys. They always hiding shit. They ass be having too much shit in the closet for me. I'on need no nucca that be in the mirror more than me. You can have them muthafuckas all to your gotdamn self."

"Kurt not like that, baby girl. It ain't shit I don't know 'bout his ass," she assures.

"I guess so. You paying a pretty penny fo' that pretty boy mutha."

"What eva. How far is the party?" Blair jumps back off the subject 'cause she knows Rena peeped her card. If she wasn't loaded with her husband's green heads, Kurt wouldn't have given her the time of day. In any case she got'em. She plans to do whatever it takes to keep his ass too.

She let him go hang out wit' his boys for a couple days. He told her ass they needed to cut the umbilical cord for at

least three days. She hesitated but she agreed after he threw that dick on her ass.

They drive up to the party, find a parking space. Rena parks the car.

"Come on, girl, it's party time," Rena shoots, freshening up her makeup.

Chapter 9

Blair, along with Rena, enter the party.

"Girl, this joint rocking. Look at all these nuccas in here!" Rena blurts, hurrying to the bar.

"I see."

"Damn right you see. What you drinking? I know not no dag on Zombies."

"Fuck you in yo ass without KY, bitch," Blair spits.

"Sound good to me."

"Rena you ain't shit. Get me a Sprite," she demands.

The both of them scope out the place. Blair nudges Rena with her elbow.

"What, you see a fine ass man? Where he at?" Rena replies.

"She's remarkably beautiful." Blair takes notice of this girl talking to some other girls at the larger bar across from her.

"Where? Who you talkin 'bout?" Rena searches.

"That girl right there with that long Nicole Miller dress on."

"Blair, unless you telling me you gay, I can't believe you just interrupted me making eye contact wit' this fine older brotha over there. Now I ain't J, the bitch is striking. She's what you call exceptional, just like us. But I'm going to get this dick. Bye." Rena high tails it to the man she's admiring.

"She had to have had a lot of surgery. She's fine from her hair to toe. Even her feet gorgeous. I don't eva want that bitch ta run into my man on them streets," she tells Rena, not realizing Rena ass done did an Audi 5,000.

Blair walks over to the lady at the bar. She has to get to know her. Maybe she can tell me what doctor she uses.

"Hello y'all, my name is Blair," says Blair to the three girls.

"Hi, Blair. I'm Sasha."

"And I'm Cody and this is Serena. Nice to meet you," Cody says. Serena says nothing. She's not feeling Blair off the rip.

"Are you all from around here?" Blair petitions.

"None of us but Sasha. The pretty one is," Cody answers.

"Don't pay her no mind. I'm an average woman." She's being humble as always.

"Blair, are you from around here?" Cody throws it back in her ball court.

"No, I'm from Costa Rica. I'm here visiting my friend. She found herself a dance partner and left me. You know how that goes."

"No we don't," Serena says, being smart.

Sasha shoots her a don't do it look.

They look at one another about Blair saying she was from Cost Rica. No accent, they thinking, but who cares, they don't plan on adding her to the circle anyway.

"Sasha, I was noticing the rich color of your hair." Blair is really being sincere.

"That would be my father's fault. He's pure Indian. My mother she's part Indian and black."

"So that makes you black," Blair schools, being envious of her.

"It would. And I'm proud of it."

The other ladies glare at one another like where did that come from.

Blair turns, looking for Rena. She sees this dude she thinks she remembers. He's flashing in her head.

"Oh shit!" Her body quivers.

"You ok?" Sasha asks.

"I'm ... I'm fine. Sasha, can I get your information. I would love to keep in touch wit' you."

"Sure." Sasha digs in her purse, pulls out her card, hands it to Blair. "Call me anytime."

"Thanks, nice meeting you all. Please excuse me. I see someone I know."

"Nice meeting you too," they all voice.

Blair approaches the man she remembers barely. "Hi, you remember me?" Blair asks him as he sits at the bar.

"Sho do. You remember me?" he asks, throwing shade.

"From the party in DC," she lets him know.

"That would be me."

Her insides are raging, moving closer to him, "Is it somewhere we can go and finish it off so that this time I'll remember who you are all the way?"

"Hell to the yeah." He's smiling from ear to ear now. "Follow me."

She does just that.

"You gon' give me some head this time?" He laughs like shit funny.

She nods yes as they stand in a small dark room.

He hurries, pulling his Johnson out. Bending down on her knees she takes hold of it by the head. He leans his head back, closing his eyes. She spits on it, massages it back and forth. He gets hard.

"You like that so far baby?" she asks in a sexy tone.

"Yes, just suck it for me."

"Ok."

She holds the head of his dick steady. All of a sudden he opens his eyes, looking down in a panic.

"*Ashhhhhhhh,* shit shit this bitch ahhhhh!"

"If you tell, I got the video of you raping me!" she yells, holding half his dick she just made into a banana split.

He's running, yelling, holding the other part of his penis. "She cut my dick, my dick!"

His boys look on. It's so dark they can't see the blood that drips throughout the place. They think he's clowning around.

"Call 911 please. Call 911!"

Blair runs out searching for Rena. Spotting her she runs over, grabs her by her arm. "We gotta go we gotta go!"

"We just got here. What you doing, what's wrong?"

"Just c'mon, we gotta go!" she yells over the music.

Rena gets the hint and they're ghost. Blair fills her in on the way to the hotel. She even shows her half his dick she dropped down in her bag.

Rena laughs. "It served his ass right, raper boy. Now he can't rape nobody else, how about that," she lets out. "Suppose he tell?" She's nervous for her friend.

"And if he do, I'll show the tape. They won't give me much if any time for it. Lorena Bobbitt didn't get no time for it."

"You sho nuff right about that."

"What you gon' do with that little ass thing," Rena adds, still laughing.

"I'ma flush the bitch."

"You ruined a good ass back though."

"It's ok. I can order another," Blair tells her, feeling good about what she just done. She's so glad she keeps a razor in the roof of her mouth. Kurt taught her that one.

Chapter 10

"You been gone it seems like for eva. What you be doing when you all the way in Jamaica, boy? I know them women be on yo ass," Simone states, standing at her sink washing dishes. "I'll be glad when you fix this dishwasher or buy us a new one, shit I get tired of washing all these dishes," she complains.

"Why you ain't buy one wit' them ends I just sent you?" Kurt strikes back, creeping up on her.

"I put that in a fund for our son. Somebody gotta think wit' they big head around here. Our son going to college, he not gon' be like his father winning the hoes over wit' his big dick, hell no."

"He gon' be shootin' hoops. That's what he gon' be doing. He gon' get drafted before college so no need for that fund, you heard," Kurt lets out.

"You say," she utters.

Kurt stands behind her lifting her robe up, drops his pants and boxers, spits on his hand, rubs it on his erect

dick, guiding it to the hole of her ass. He pushes his head in slowly, moving her long 24-inch hair to the side, bending forward turning his neck sideways he sinks his teeth in both sides of her small neck.

"Ummm uh," she moans, closing her pretty eyes, dropping the dish that's in her hand into the sudsy water concentrating only on him.

"It feels good? You miss papa?" he groans, releasing her neck.

"Um hum," she moans in lust.

Pushing more in sliding back and forth, biting down harder this time, the pain shoots through her body. She can't feel the pain of his massive dick 'cause of the pain he's delivering on her neck. Pushing his whole dick in her ass, riding, pumping, grinding, clamping his fingers down on her nipples tight as he can.

"Um shit um fuck." He pumps, throwing his dick in-out. She's cumming down her legs, massive amounts of cum gushing like water.

He loves it.

"Cum Simone, cum for papa."

She does nonstop. He ain't neva had a woman like her that cums so much. He loves her pussy.

Riding her phat ass harder, he pulls her arms backward.

"Who ass is dis, bitch?"

"Yours Kurt, yours." Slinging that dick she loves so much up in her, she yells out, "Fuck me! Fuck me nigga like I'm yo only bitch fuck this pussy!"

"Shit, I'm getting there bae," his ass groans.

Pulling out sticking his shitty dick in her pussy, thick milky cum pours instantly, covers his dick, adding his nut to hers.

"Got fuckin damn you BITCH!" he yells, busting off up in her. Pulling his dick out, he drips cum on the floor looking down.

"Fuck Simone you made a whole puddle. How you be doing dat, yo? I'ing neva seen no bitch cum like you do. A whole puddle dat there is porn star shit."

She smiles. "I want some more, nucca." She hops up on him. He carries her to the room. They start all over again.

Chapter 11

Mrs. Scott enters the panic room with her daughter on her heels. They find Shawn watching TV.

Mrs. Scott has been working with Shawn around the clock. He's motivated, wanting full mobility. With the assistance of a walker he still can't walk. His talking abilities have not come back yet. He still has to wear Pampers as well. The fact that he can walk some makes him wanna push harder.

Mrs. Scott and Sasha move in closer to him.

"Shawn, this my daughter Sasha."

"Hi Shawn, nice to meet you," Sasha greets with her hand out.

He shakes it, nodding at her.

"Shawn, she's a licensed Neurologist at John Hopkins hospital in Baltimore," her mother informs.

She's stunning as fuck. He's thinking to himself, *I can't believe my luck.*

Sasha is just what she said—half black/Indian. She looks somewhat like J.Lo but she has deep green eyes, 30 inches of long cold black hair, she's 5'7" about 150 pounds 36-23-34, she works out so her body is cut up, six pack abs arms and legs cut up as well. She doesn't look hard though. She still has that softness about her. Her skin complexion is a bronzy glow as if she goes to the tanning booth, but she doesn't—it's all hers.

Shawn wants desperately to reach out and touch. *His mind plays tricks on him. Now Shawn you gotta get better. Nobody wants a cripple,* he thinks while staring at her.

Only if he knew she's not like that, she's the real deal.

"Shawn was poisoned. Antifreeze. Someone tried to kill him. Well his ex-wife, truth be told. He said she was raped by one of his old buddies. He didn't want to go to jail for murdering him so he let it be, plus the man saved his life at one time. She didn't like the fact that he didn't do anything to him so she tried to kill him after she killed his buddy," her mother explains.

"My God!" Sasha let out, touching him on his arm.

"Shawn, I want her to examine you to see what she can do to help you."

He nods ok.

"Shawn, can I take a MRI of your body? I have to read your nerves, if you don't mind. My mother told me you had her buy a MRI machine and an X-Ray machine as well. You're really spending a lot of money when I can do all these things at the hospital cheaper," Sasha tells him.

Picking up a pen and paper he writes, *I don't wanna go out too much so it's cool. I got the money can you do it here?*

"Sure we can. You want to take it tomorrow I will have to get the die so I can see your nerves better."

That'a work, he writes.

"Tomorrow it is. I'll be here after work," Sasha assures.

"Shawn, I'ma walk her to the door. I'll be back to cook you some good food, then we can go to work," her mother tells him.

He nods, waving Sasha off, smiling at Sasha. He wants her but don't know if she's too far outta range for'em.

Chapter 12

The Next Day

Sasha took an MRI of Shawn's body.

"Shawn, I have good news. We can do an operation on you so that you will be able to talk again. You have two nerves that are connecting where they shouldn't be. If I can separate them it'll start your speech signals flowing again. Then you will be able to talk and eventually walk on your own. My mother has taken you as far as she can. Shawn, the bad news is you'll have to come to the hospital for this."

He nods ok.

"Good, I will set it up."

Sasha calls her office then another doctor. They set the date 2 weeks from today. She ends her call, bends over, kisses him on his cheek.

"Sorry this happened to you. We'll get you back to normal soon. Trust me, but trust more in God."

Shawn will trust her before God. He's mad at Him right now.

He nods again ok.

"Bye, I'll see you soon," she tells him.

Her mother walks her to the door. "Sasha, this man has a shit load of money. His father left it to him. He was a dope dealer and a pimp. I remember him from school but his grandfather had money anyway," her mother yawks, standing at the front door of his house.

"That's a good thing, mom. Then he can pay for all this, or I don't know what he would've done."

"I know. It's a true blessing," her mother agrees with her.

"He seems to be such a nice person. He's very good looking. I mean *very* good looking. It's a shame what happened to him. I'll get him on track, you'll see. He'll be as good as new. Mom, I know God is pleased with your work. You did a good job."

"You know baby that's all that matters to me. Shawn tries to pay me. I tell him no, God will take care of me. It's a gift. I have a job, you know," her mother tells her, starting to cry.

"I know, mom. Stop crying. He will be delighted once he gets well. You'll see."

"He's such a good fella," she tells her daughter, not knowing those two last words are so true.

"I see that, mom. I do." She doesn't get what Sasha is saying but Sasha knows all too well the signs of a Good Fella.

Chapter 13

"I'm here. I know I'm late but I'm here." Cody strolls over to Sasha as she sits at the dining table in Martin's Steaks House.

"You're late. Like 20 minutes late. You need to get yourself a scheduler," Sasha expresses.

"I'm here. Did you order yet?"

"Yes, for both of us. The usual."

"Good, I'm starving."

"Cody?" Sasha calls her best friend's name.

"Yes?" Cody answers, rubbing her hands together as the waiter places the food on the table. She grabs her fork, ready to dig in.

"You going to say grace?" Sasha asks.

"Forgot. Go."

Sasha says the grace. Cody has one eye open like how long you gon' thank God for the damn food. When she says Amen, Cody digs in.

"I thought the damn food was gon' get cold, that long ass grace."

"Girl, eat. You so greedy."

"Tell me what you was gon' say before the waiter came," Cody says, chopping down on her steak.

"*Well* … I met this man."

"You meet a lot of men. What makes this one so special? Did something happen? Can you pass the salt?" Cody utters.

"He's nice looking, even more so he's nice to me."

Cody stops chewing. "He's nice looking? Really, like how? You want to date him or you just think he's nice looking?" She's baffled. Her friend doesn't talk about men much. Most of the time she's talking about work.

"I think I would like to see him. More of him."

Cody starts chewing again.

"He needs surgery. He was poisoned. It left him unable to talk or walk. Mother, she's helping him. She has it where he can walk with a walker."

"So you telling me you like a cripple? That's what you trying to tell me?" she articulates, moving her lips slowly.

"I don't care about that. That's not a positive word. None of us are perfect."

"Sorry, get your patties out a bunch. Boy you do like him. Where he live?"

"Get this, he's only like in his 20's. He's loaded. He has his own houses, car, money all of it. Mom grew up with his father."

"Don't tell me he's a Jehovah witness too. Man I get enough of that wit' your mother. *Whoo*, please tell me he's not."

"Stop it, no he's not. He's Muslim. His father was a pimp/hustler selling drugs," Sasha explains.

Cody eyes her.

"Don't judge. That don't make him one," Sasha voices.

"It damn sho don't mean he's one, but I need you to be careful 'cause you my friend."

"I will. One more thing …"

"Don't tell me he cross dresses."

"You funny. I like that one, but no. I think I already love him."

"So this is why you treating me to my favorite restaurant. So you can get my blessing?" Cody asks.

"Kinda sorda."

"You have it. Live your life. You only live once. Can you pass me the steak sauce? For some reason it's kinda dry today."

Chapter 14

I'm so bored. I really should go check on my husband, but what if the police are there. I haven't heard anything but you never know. I think I'll let someone discover him. I'll just tell them we were thinking about getting divorced, she thinks to herself as she finishes up her hair, glancing in the mirror of the bathroom. *Blair, you're so beautiful. I'm so conceited, nothing wrong wit' that though.*

Snatching up her Louis V bag, she opens it. "Shit, I forgot about you." She lays hands on the half of penis she kept. She goes to the bathroom and flushes it down the toilet, watching it go down. She smiles. "You won't rape nobody else, will you?" she says to herself.

She starts cleaning her bag out. She comes across Sasha's card.

"Um, I wonder what you're doing today, Ms. Sasha Scoot." She apprehends her mobile, dialing the number on the card. "I need to change my group of friends. I need people that think like me that's smart with money," she says out loud.

"Hello?"

"Hello to you, Sasha. This is Blair. We met last night, remember?"

"Oh yes Blair, how are you?"

"I'm good, in spite of that episode."

"What episode?"

"That guy running through the crowd talking about how somebody cut his private part off."

"Oh yes that was weird, wasn't it?"

"Yes. I left, it was too weird for me." Blair plays it off well.

"Me too. We all left when the paramedics came. Someone really sliced half his groin off. He said he couldn't remember who before he passed out," Sasha explains.

"I bet his mind must have been on nothing but his incident. Anyway, I called to see what you're into today."

"I'm with my friend eating right now, but I'm clear later after 5."

"How about legal Seafood downtown 6:30 tonight, my treat," Blair assures.

"I can't turn down a good meal."

"See you there."

"See you then," Sasha says, surprised Blair even called.

Sasha is really a kindhearted person. She's open to everyone. She has lots of friends, Cody being her best friend. She lost her only sister to AIDS. She killed herself

on her college campus. That tore Sasha apart. A day don't go by that she doesn't think about her. Her sister and her were not close at all so this makes her feel guilty that she never got to talk to her before she killed herself.

Sasha has never been touched by a man before. She's so into her career. It keeps her busy. However when she met Shawn she felt a tingle somewhere she's never felt before. She can't get her mind off him. She told her mother she's coming over to talk wit' Shawn after her lunch with Cody today. Her mother found that odd but she put it off thinking she just wants to help Shawn.

Chapter 15

Shawn's operation went well. He's been working hard, making a major comeback. He's talking well, his vocals are strong. His weight is fully back, his chest is buff. He has an eight pack, his body is on point for sho. Shawn is able to walk on his own. Shawn works out for hours throughout the day. If Blair were to see him she would not recognize him at all. Sasha has been by his side day after day. They joke around a lot, they also play lots of board games. She really likes being around him.

To him, she is so smart. He never thought he could date a doctor. He's never been attracted to older women but he's loving it.

Mrs. Scott doesn't come by as often. When she does she cooks for Shawn. He loves her cooking. Southern food at its best.

Occasionally Shawn leaves the house. Not too often. He doesn't want to risk running into someone that knows

him. He wants to be 100% before going around the people that care for him. They don't know where he is. They think he's MIA with his wife who they never see. Kurt makes sure he's never with Blair when they come to DC. He doesn't want any of the crew to see him with her. If they knew what Blair was doing they would kill her, then Kurt, even though he knows nothing. He just thinks she left Shawn for him. He doesn't plan on staying with Blair. He's just using her to get on his feet the way he wants to. Blair told him that her and Shawn are divorced and he paid her alimony. He told her he was leaving town for a minute. This he can believe 'cause at his party in Vegas that night he told them he was getting out the game. Shawn, commander, took over. For now he wonders if Shawn has lost his mind by not contacting him, not answering his line. For now he says he'll just make shit happen until Shawn comes around to calling him. None of them know about the Fort Washington home. Shawn keeps his private life just that private.

Sasha and Shawn sit, enjoying a game of *Trouble*.

"Gotcha. Go back, take yo fine ass all the way back!" Shawn yells, landing his man on hers, sending her back to start.

"You got me boo, but the game not over yet. I got two more men out there. The fat lady ain't sing," she says, frustrated. She hates to lose.

"Can we just stretch out in front the fireplace, you in my arms or some'em?" He put it out there.

Sasha blushes. "That I would love to do."

He puts a pile of pillows by the fireplace. Sasha puts in an old movie, *Coming To America.* They lay watching, laughing. Once the move is over, Sasha eyes Shawn while in his arms.

"Shawn?"

"Yeah, bae."

"How you feel?"

"Great."

"I do too," she lets out, smiling,

He kisses her on her lips. She receives him. Their kisses grow heated. She climbs her phat ass on top of'em, removing her shirt.

"No," he says, breaking their embrace.

She looks at him, not understanding. "No?" she repeats, in her feelings though.

"Sasha, I want you so bad you gotta believe dat baby fo' sho. I really want yo ass. Us laying it down, that shit is nothing to me. I can get ass anytime, anywhere. Had lots of it. You know I married a gold diggin' bitch, nothing to hide about that. This time I want something different. I want love. I want it without lust, sex, all that shit. It clouds the mind. I want to really get to know you, everything about you if that is possible. If I tap that ass you'll fall in love for all

the wrong reasons. Or it may be me falling for all the wrong reasons. I don't want you to feel just that about me, about us. Sex wears off. Intimacy is up here." He points to his head. "That lasts forever, that's something I've never had. I can whack my shit off anytime but to have a woman, a real woman such as yourself that's right there … I want to last longer than anything, feel me?"

Gladly eyeing him, "Shawn, that really really feels good to hear you say. I thought you just wanted sex. I didn't want that to come between us. I wanted to make you happy."

"You make me happy by being here. You're the reason I can talk and walk well; you and your mother, needless to say. I learn from you, all that slang talk out the window because of you, well some of it. Smile. Sasha, I want you to know a nigga love you. I wanna fall in love wit' you though. That there is hella real talk."

She stares straight in his face. "Shawn, I love you. I want you to know I'm in this for the long haul."

"Baby, that's good to know. Now what movie you want to watch this time?" He gives her the option again.

"*Scarface*, nucca." She laughs 'cause she's talking slang.

"Now that there is my man, Tony Montana," he lets out, smiling, retrieving the movie.

Chapter 16

"Over here." Blair waves, sitting at the dining table of the Ritz-Carlton restaurant located in Pentagon City, VA.

She stands, greeting Sasha by wrapping her arms around her. This is their first time meeting up with one another since they met at the party that night. They set a date before; however, Sasha was called to an emergency at the hospital.

"Blair, how you been?" Sasha says.

"I'm doing well. Thanks for asking."

"Shall we?" Sasha says, asking permission to sit down and eat.

They take their seats. The waiter comes over, writes their orders down. The both of them order Lobster fried rice with a Singapore Sling cocktail. They look at one another giggling.

"That's funny," Blair speaks up. "We like the same food and drink," Blair blurts out, remembering the drink Sasha ordered at the party that night.

"It's funny. You never know, huh?" Sasha responds.

"You never know. So what you been up to, Ms. busy?" Blair asks.

"Working my butt off. Being a doctor is a lot of work when you work for a hospital," Sasha explains. "And you, what you been up too?"

"Traveling. My husband loves to travel," Blair lies as usual.

"What was it you said you did?" Sasha is digging.

"I didn't, but I'm a Politic Attorney."

"Now that sounds like a lot of fun."

"Your meals, ladies," the waiter chimes in.

"Thanks," they say in sync.

They eat, talk politics. Sasha is starting to warm up to Blair, seeing as though she knows so much about government law, one of Sasha's favorite subjects when she was in school.

In the middle of their conversation her cell rings. Sasha takes notice of the number.

"Excuse me. I have to take this."

"Sure," Blair says, hawking her food.

She walks away from the table, answering the call.

"Hey my best friend," Sasha greets.

"Hey back to you," Cody shoots. "You popped in my mind. I just wanted to check up on you, that's all."

"I'm fine. I'm here with that lady Blair. The one we met at the par—"

Cody cuts in. "I remember her. What type of person is she?"

"She seems to be nice. She's an attorney, politics at that."

"She didn't strike me as an attorney. Then again you never can judge a book by its cover, right? It's good to see you making more friends, but keep her on your end. I don't need no more friends."

"Cody, you're so mean. Stop it."

"I'll let you get back to your date."

"I'll call you later when I leave," Sasha tells her.

"Love you. Be careful. Don't be telling her all your business," Cody commands.

"Now you know better than that. You're the only one I talk to about my problems."

"Lata," Cody lets out.

"The same to ya."

She returns to the table. "I apologize. That was my good friend. Now where were we?"

"No problem. You're probably cold by now."

They start chopping it up again. After they eat they sit at the bar, drink sodas, having a good time. Sasha feels she's met a good person, someone that she thinks she can let in her circle.

Blair glances at her watch. "It's getting late. We need to get going, don't you think?"

"You're right. I'll pay for the sodas, you paid for the meal. That's only fair," Sasha insists.

"You got it," Blair tells her.

Sasha whips out her American Black Card. Blair is a little envious but she knows hanging with people like Sasha that is something she will have to get used to.

Chapter 17

Shawn and Sasha move past the many stores at PG Plaza.

"You wanna hit up food court before we go?" he asks.

"How did you know my belly was screaming food please feed me?" she says with laughter.

"I just guess since I'm hungry too. After we grub I wanna take you to meet someone that's special to me."

"I thought I was the only special person in your life," she says, glowing. Gazing into his eyes, "I'll love to meet your special person as long as the person not going to take you away from me."

"Never that. No one can do that. You'on know that by know?"

She bats her eyes as they walk over to the food court. They order, eat, then Shawn drives her to a community in Englewood development located in Chesapeake, VA.

"This community is breathtaking. My goodness. It must cost a fortune to stay here?" she comments as they pass the water boats and nice houses.

"I know, right. It's like Wonderland," he makes reference.

They arrive in front of the house he comes to visit, turning off the engine. "We're here," he sighs.

"Why you seem nervous?"

He hunches his shoulders. "Let's go in."

They walk up the steps, come to a halt. He rings the doorbell.

"Coming. Hold on," the person on the other end voices, opening the door.

"My God. I thought it was your voice," says a lady dressed to kill, wearing a blue and white wrap-around Givenchy summer dress that hangs to her feet. She invites them in.

"Close the door, Shawndale. You two have a seat. I gotta go feed Strong Hold."

Sasha hawk eyes Shawn.

"Strong Hold is her dog. It's a Pitt," he explains.

"Oh," she remarks.

They take a seat in the family room. Shawn turns on the TV.

"You want something to drink?" he asks Sasha.

"Boy, you act like this your house."

"It is, kinda. I just don't live in it," he comments, cutting a slice of coconut cream pie from the fridge, stuffing his face. He grabs a soda from the pop cooler.

"You sure?" He offers one more time, holding up the pie. "This shit good. I'm telling you she's the best baker on the east coast."

"Shawn, we just ate. I'm still stuff."

"You missing out."

"You greedy as hell," Sasha tells him.

"I apologize. I had to feed him. You know how he gets around. So what brings you over here? I haven't seen you in like six months or so."

"Sorry, I been busy," Shawn lies.

She looks over at Sasha. "Now who do I owe the pleasure of accompanying my son in visiting me?"

Sasha becomes confused real quick.

"Her name is Sasha. Sasha, this my ma Mary."

"Hello, Ma'am. Nice to meet you." *I thought his mother was dead,* Sasha is thinking. *I don't like being lied to.*

"Sasha, you must be special to Shawndale. He never brings ladies to see me. As a matter of fact, he never brings anyone to meet me." She turns to Shawn. "Did you come to tell me I'm going to be a grandmother or you two getting married?"

"Ma! See, dis why you never meet nobody."

His mother becomes confused. "I apologize. Did I say something wrong?" Her face has the look of embarrassment.

"No, Ma, you didn't. I love you." Shawn hugs her tight around her neck, kissing her forehead.

"Ma, this pie is like the best," he says, changing the subject.

"I just made it. You want some, Sasha?" she offers.

"Sure, I'll take a piece." Being a doctor Sasha sees something's not adding up with her. She's sure Shawn will explain later. So she takes the pie.

Chapter 18

It's 11 at night. Shawn and Sasha say their goodbyes to his mother who sees them to the car.

"Nice to meet you, Ma'am," Sasha says.

"Likewise," his mother replies.

Shawn kisses her. "Bye. I'll be back next week. By the way, the garden looks good. You staying busy, I see."

"Yes, Shawndale, stop worrying I'm fine."

"Ma, that's my job. I will always worry about my queen," he lets out.

She pats his back. "Get going, it's getting late. Bye now." She waves, standing on the curb as they pull off.

"Shawn, I thought you said your mother was dead?" Sasha asks before they could hit the corner.

"The lady that raised me is dead. My father had two women—my real mother and my stepmother. My stepmother, she raised me like I was her own. I wouldn't have known the difference until my father told me at the age of 12 about my real mother."

"Oh, why you didn't tell me? Are you overprotective of her? And she's never met your wife, or ex-wife should I say. Why is that?"

"Nah, she never met her. My mother has Schizophrenia. When she takes her meds she's fine, but when she don't it's all downhill so I don't bring people around her 'cause I neva know. Sasha, she was sick. My father and her didn't see eye to eye. He didn't understand what was wrong with'a. She would beat me then turn on my father. She thought we were spying on her. She would say shit like she worked for the Army and she had to kill us. One day she duct taped me and locked me in the closet. My father looked all over for me that day. When he found me he told her she had to go."

"Why didn't he get her help?"

"I just told you he didn't know what was wrong back then. You know how it was. They didn't have the technology they have now. My father was 74 and my mother is 69. She just looks young. They had me when they were older. That's why I'm the only child."

"That explains the small hospital I seen at the end of the complex."

"It's just for the people in that complex. All of them have mental problems," he informs.

"Shawn, that's awesome."

"I found out about the place through this broad I used ta date. She did a lot for me. She neva met my moms but I told her about the situation and now my mother is safe."

"You really love her, don't you?"

"Hell yeah. Don't you love yo moms?"

"I do, but I'm not protective over her like you are over yours."

"I gotta be. She's all I have. Now you are too."

Sasha smiles. That warms her heart. She's so in love with Shawn. He's the perfect man in her eyes.

He swings his car in front her house.

"Dis you. I'll call you in the morning," he tells her.

"Oh ok, then you drive careful." She can't believe he's not coming in for a minute.

He gives her a long passionate kiss, then he separates his lips from hers.

"I love you, Shawn."

"I love you too," he tells her, wondering why his dick not hard dough.

Chapter 19

Kurt is doing so good. He flipped the money Blair gave him. He's back wit' Shawn's old crew as their supplier this time. He convinced Shawn's boy to get their weight from him. Kurt's glad he made that move.

He sits on the beach in his swim trunks at Blair's newest home located in St. Lucia Island Coconut Bay. He eyeballs Blair as she comes out the water.

"This is nice, ain't it?" Blair utters, standing in front of her man reaching for her towel.

"It's ok. It's not DC dough," he confirms, looking up at her, squinting his eyes from the sun.

"You don't like it here?" she asks, drying off with her LV beach towel.

Placing his hand over his forehead protecting it from the sun, "Blair, dis not gon' work. I'm not in love wit' you at all."

Blair's face changes from chipper to a look of defeat. She stops drying off, placing her hand on her hip.

"Kurt, what you mean you not in love wit' me?! What we been doing, just playing house? Or are you playing me?!"

"I'on know, I guess playin' house. I love you, B. You a good girl but I'm just not in love wit' you, feel me?"

"You love somebody else, your baby momma huh?"

He lifts up, brushing the sand off his trunks. "No, that's not it. You not loyal, Blair. You left my man to fuck with me, at least that's what you tell me. I'm not built to live like dis. It's not right. Shawn did a lot for a nigga. I owe him loyalty, more than this for sho. You ain't got dat," he spits, making his way back to the beach house where his clothes are already packed with his one-way ticket back to DC.

She follows him, her heart busted. "Kurt, please don't do this. What I'ma do without you?" she begs.

"B, you're a beautiful, sexy, smart, rich lady. My boy Shawn set you up sweet. You'll get lots of men, trust dat."

"How long you been planning your escape, nigga?!"

He chuckles. "You funny. My escape? I just realize I made a big mistake. I gotta go, that's all." He grabs his bags, locks eyes with Blair's. "You'll be fine I promise. Take it easy."

He turns for the door.

"You broke ass nigga I took good care of yo ass. Who gon' want you?! Who gon' pay your child support?! How yo bitch ass gon' make it?!"

He turns around, facing her. "Who gon' want me? Lots of bitches. How I'ma pay my child support? The same way I been paying, by throwing this dick around." He swigs his leg back and forth, laughing, making an about face reaching for the knob.

She picks up a glass bowl nearest her, throws it at the door as it closes behind him.

"*Oooh!* You monkey nut fucka!" she yells.

Chapter 20

Shawn arrives at Sasha's house. He rings the doorbell. She answers.

"Hot damn, is this the right house or am I dreaming!" he voices, standing in her door watching her sexy body.

She's dressed in an all red sheer gown.

"No, you at the right place. What you gon' do wit it?" she puts out there, tired of him playing around wit' her.

Not wanting to turn her down again, he moves in closer, laying hands on her small hips, shutting the door with the back of his foot, kissing her on her soft lips, walking her towards the guest room located right beside them. He gently pushes her on the queen size bed, dropping his clothes on the floor, in addition he moves in, raising her gown up.

With a watchful eye on hers, "Is this what you want?" he asks, lowering his head between her legs, placing his wet tongue on her clit.

She moans softly. *"Hum ... ye ... sss."* She arches her back, placing her hand on the top of his head.

Shawn draws circles around the lips of her kitty cat, sucking all her moistness. She starts digging her hands into the sheets.

"I love you. I love you so much I do," she pronounces. Her heart beats faster as he lifts her up, places his penis at the opening of her vagina.

"You on the pill?" he whistles.

"Uh-huh," she lies.

He starts pulling on his meat. It seems that it won't get hard. But she continues to moan, not wanting to lose the moment.

"Uh-huh."

He goes back to eating her pussy until she has an orgasm, then he lays on top of her for a minutes. He lifts up.

"Sorry, bae, I don't know what's wrong. My shit just didn't wanna get up."

"It's ok. It happens. You've been through a lot. It'll happen one day, you'll see." She tries making him feel good about himself.

He turns, holding her thinking, *What in the fuck? I never had that happen. Is it her or me?*

Chapter 21

"I can't believe Kurt did this to me. Rena, what was I to his ass, chop liver? He played me to the core, like I'ma fool!" Blair says into the phone.

"What made him lie, Blair? What he got, another woman or some shit?" Rena questions.

"I asked him was he going to go back wit' his baby mommas. That son of a bitch said no, it's not that. He just don't love me. He claims he can't trust me. But get this, why wasn't he saying that when I was spending all that doe on his ass!"

"Why can't he trust you? What made him say that?" Rena is trying to process it all.

"I'on fuckin know. Your guess is as good as mines. I guess it's because he's my ex-husband's boy, but you know that's a crap of shit. Hell, if that's the case why he fuck wit' me in the first place, right?"

"Maybe it's true. Maybe he feels guilty all of a sudden. You should too. I mean your ex did just get out the hospital

not too long ago. Y'all filed for a divorce, you say. Then you started fucking his boy, that's low down. I wouldn't like that shit if I was Shawn. It just looks like you thirsty as hell right now."

"What you mean? You saying you don't believe Shawn filed for a divorce from me?"

"Well it does sound crazy. Why would he? He needs you about now. But you my girl so if you say he did I'ma ride wit' you." Rena is trying to make sense of it all still.

"I guess you got a point, but I love Kurt. And for the record Shawn did file."

"You don't have to convince me. I don't know about Kurt's love for you but Shawn I do know loves you. Blair, you just have to give him a chance to prove himself. We all fuck up sometimes. We not perfect, none of us. He's a good man."

"You right," Blair tells her, really thinking about it now that Kurt dumped her. "Rena, I did lie. You my girl I can't front no more wit' you. He didn't file. I did leave him for Kurt. I fucked up for real. I was still in my feelings about him not taking care of his boy Jazz after he found out what he did to me. When he was in the hospital suffering I was happy when I picked him up. I hated him for it so I thought I would get with one of his boys to get back at'em. Kurt was easy, his dick was off the chain. I was wrong. Now what do I do? I substituted my love for Shawn to Kurt. Look what happened—I got hurt again," she explains, starting to tear up.

"I know 'cause you was never over Shawn. He was the first man you ever loved and who loved you. You need to go back home to'em are my thoughts," Rena coaches.

Blair starts crying, thinking about how she left that man for dead. How she really does love'em, how she wish he was alive about now.

"Rena, I do love Shawn. I do but how do I forgive him how?!'

"You just do. Cry that shit out and go get your fine ass money man."

"But suppose he'on want me?"

"The way that nucca was about you, he will. I saw it in his eyes. Y'all just went through a lot of drama in the beginning. Some do and some in the end just forgive him and move on for it. Life is what you make it. Go back to your man. All this trippin' and runnin' you doing is from being hurt. Blair, go fight for what's yours. It ain't too many men like Shawn."

Only if she knew he might be dead, she thinks to herself while Rena continues to school her.

"I love you, Rena. Thanks for being a friend and for not judging me."

"I would neva do that, my hoe ass please. Look at me, Blue just walked in. You gon' be ok?"

"You know this always. I'm on my way back to DC to claim what's mines," Blair tells her.

"Good, that's the Blair I know. Drop by to see me when you get here, ok?"

"You know I will. Love you friend."

"I love you too girl," Rena says, hanging up the phone.

Chapter 22

One full week has passed since Shawn and Sasha's love-making experience gone wrong. The two of them have grown closer. They've gotten to know one another better. Sasha is head over heels in love with Shawn. She can hardly work, all she thinks about is her new man who treats her like a princess even though his dick won't seem to get up for her. She chalks that up to him being paralyzed before. The candy, roses, teddy bears he sends her makes up for all that. He even has things delivered to her job, which means bragging rights for her. Sometimes he has them delivered to the front door of her house. She's so happy she lost her virginity to a man like Shawn. This is how she dreamed it.

She went to see his mother without him two days ago. She didn't tell'em because his mother told her she wanted it to be their little secret. She likes Sasha a lot. She introduced her to some of her other friends. Sasha doesn't mind at all. She understands what they're going through; after all, she is a neurologist.

Shawn thinks he found the one. The thought of not killing Jazz continues to run across his mind. He's beating himself up for not showing Blair he was the man for her. He feels he was supposed to be her protector. She had to do a man's job all alone. That's eating him up on the inside.

He's not mad at Blair for what she did to him. He just wished she would've killed him like a real soldier as well, instead of making him suffer. Then again he's glad she didn't. He wouldn't be back. Most of all he wouldn't have met the woman of his life—Sasha.

Chapter 23

Blair exits the airport. Planting her feet back on American soil, she hails a yellow cab, puts her bags in the trunk, gets in.

"555 Riverview Dr. Fort-Washington, MD," she states, closing the door.

"Ok ma'am. How was your flight?" he asks, setting his meter.

"I rather not talk. I just wanna get to my destination."

"You're the boss."

The cab driver pulls into busy traffic making his way to her home. Making a stop at the red light, "Nice car," he says out loud, talking to himself.

Blair turns her head to observe what he is talking about. Her mouths flies open.

"Kurt, that black and mild son of a bitch!" she unknowingly yells out. *So that's the low grade he left me for.* She sees him talking, laughing with a lady. She kisses him, sitting close to him as they are being chauffeured in his new all black chromed out Maybach Mercedes G-650 priced at $550,000.

"Follow that care, Sir," she orders.

"Huh?" he lets out, looking through his rearview mirror.

"I'll pay you triple. Just follow the gotdamn car!" She's lit.

The driver does what he's being paid for. The driver lands them in Potomac, MD.

"Stop right here." He stops a few houses back.

The neighborhood is stunning. The house looks like a ten-million-dollar mansion. Her heart thumps as she watches their chauffeur let her out the car. The two of them float into their home. The chauffeur pulls off.

"Pull closer to the house."

The cab driver obeys, scanning the grounds. Blair sees children's bikes, big wheels, all kinds of kids stuff.

On point she rings him. "Answer, you dirty dog," she voices. The cab driver smiles, feeling like a spy off TV.

'Hello?"

She's surprised he answered. "Hello you, where you at?"

"Home. Why?"

"Just asking."

"You alone?"

"No. Why again?" he asks.

"Oh just asking. A bitch can't ask? Well, who you wit'?"

"Keeping real short wit' you. My kid's mom."

"Which one?"

"The one I'm with. Yo what up Blair. Don't do this to yourself. We had fun, you was there for me. That's why I jive answered the phone."

"A bitch Gucci. I just gotta ask you why would you leave me for her. She's ugly as butt fuck."

He becomes silent as snow, wondering how she's seen her.

"You still there?" she says, smiling.

"It's not about looks. That's your problem, you all about the outside. It's the inside that counts. Hold up, why am I explaining myself to you?" he offers.

"You right, you don't owe me shit, a muthafuckin frog's ass for that matter. Here is the thing though: I know why I neva seen a picture of'a. Your kids, now that's a different story. They're so beautiful. They say beauty and the beast make some pretty children. I still say she must got some good pussy 'cause she ain't blessed in the fucken face whatsoever. Fuck that pretty on the inside shit. I gotta look at a muthafucka when I'm on my back. Fuck that, so call me what you want but you can't say my ass is ugly. And what's that black shit on the side of her face. Yuck! Please tell me it's her birthmark."

"Blair, I know you hurt. You tryna hurt me. It's not working, you making yo'self look pressed."

"Not!" she shoots off, ending the call tears flying from her eyes.

"You ok, ma'am?" the cab driver asks.

"No, take me home now," she orders one more time.

Chapter 24

The cab arrives at Blair and Shawn's pad in Fort Washington. She pays the driver what she promised—triple the fare.

"Thanks," he relays, taking the money from her soft hands.

Opening the door to the cab, she sets foot on her land. The driver pops his trunk. She retrieves her bag. Shuttling up the steps, anchoring herself in front her door, watching the cab disappear, she sticks her hand in her bag.

Do I wanna face the music? What will I find? Is he dead? What do I do? she thinks to herself, pulling her keys out the Dior bag that hangs from her slender shoulder. Sticking her key in the lock, she lays hands on her bags making her way into the dark house, moving about. She stops at the kitchen where she last left Shawn. Releasing her bags, she gasps, covering her mouth.

"Shit where is he?! Who could have him?! Oh my God, did the police come and get'em?! Why nobody call me? My card is right here above the stove. Is he really dead, did I

kill'em?! Oh My God, my God!" she yells out after standing there for about an hour, not knowing what to do. "I need to settle my nerves. A shower. I need to take a shower then maybe I can think of what to do, where to go," she says out loud. "Hell, I need a drink too." Reaching in the kitchen cabinet, "Just what I need," she lets out, admiring the bottle of Rosé.

Putting her hands on it she walks up the familiar steps, sliding in the master bedroom. She pops the cork, takes a drink from the bottle, sets it down on the dresser then starts taking her clothes off one piece at a time, moving towards the bathroom. She turns on the shower, sticking her hand in the hot steamy shower.

"Yes."

Stepping in, she takes a seat on the shower bench. Holding her head up looking at the ceiling she cries, prays, cries for her soul, for his soul, she's confused.

"Why Lord? Why am I like this? What have I done? I love Shawn. Why did I get so mad? Only if I knew what I know now," she cries out to God for the first time in a long time.

Chapter 25

Shawn reaches his house. He's so excited. He turns off his engine, embraces his mobile.

"Call Sasha," he voices into his cell.

"Calling Sasha."

"Hey there, my baby," she greets.

"I hope so. What you doing?" he asks.

"Getting ready for bed, thinking about you as always."

"Just wanted ta check up on you. Dream about me, you heard."

"And while I'm dreaming about you, sleep with the angels yourself," she tells him.

He blushes. "One mo' thing," he says.

"What's that?" she asks.

"Can I take you to breakfast in the morning?"

"Sure, can't wait. What time?"

"Six. I'll be there at six."

"I'll be waiting, looking the part."

"I bet. Goodnight again," she lets out.

"Back to you."

She blushes. He smiles, then ends the call.

"She's a good girl. Where she been all my life?" he expresses out loud, getting out the car.

He walks in the house only to hear water running upstairs. Staying calm, slowly he raises his .40 that was pressed against his hip bone. Creeping up the steps to the master bedroom he sees bags and a trail of women's clothing laying in the bathroom.

It must be Mrs. Scott, are his thoughts. As he starts making his way out the bathroom, Blair turns the water off. Stepping out, she turns the corner grabbing a towel.

"Ahhhh!" she yells, dropping the towel. She sees the back of Shawn's body walking away.

Recognizing the voice he spins around, "Blair, what the fuck?!"

"Shawn, how you—?"

"Fuck you doing in here?!" he cuts her short.

"This where I live. You still my husband—"

Cutting her off again, "Used ta be your fuckin husband!" Getting all up in her space, "What you come back for, to see if you can finish the fuckin job, huh?!"

She becomes scared but hot body in some sick way. He sees she's nervous, scared and has a loss for words. He stands in front of her nude body. Taking stock, his dick extends her way. He realizes it's nothing wrong with him after all; it's just that Blair is the woman he longs for. He still loves her sick deranged ass.

The woman that tried to kill his ass he's still in love wit'.

Abruptly he takes hold of her face. Sticking his tongue down her throat, she returns the greeting. He drops his sweatpants to his feet, his boxers follow, kicking them to the side.

He scoops her up, carries her to the bed, then fucks the shit outta her like she's the first piece of ass he's ever had.

When they both reach a climax of love, silence fills the air. A look of understanding settles on their faces. Shawn releases her, turns over. She lays her head on his manly chest. They fall asleep balled up together—a sleep of true peace.

Chapter 26

The Next Day

Buzz ... buzzzzz. Shawn's cell alerts him over and over.

"Shit, what time is it?" He rolls over glaring at the clock and his cell that sits on his night stand that's beside his king size bed.

"It's 7, what the fuck?" He looks over at Blair. His phone buzzes again.

Stretching out, he puts his phone to his ear. "Hello?" he whispers.

"You ok? You forgot to pick me up. I've been waiting since 6 this morning; it's 7 now!" Sasha screams on'em all in one breath.

In a morning fog, "Hello?" he says again.

"Shawn, did you hear what I just said?" She's getting pissed all over again.

"Hey." He turns to his left, getting out the bed, making his way to the bathroom. Blair rolls over, moaning. "Sasha, can I call you right back. I'm sorry. I'll hit you right back."

"Oh, ok then," she says, confused. "Is everything ok with you?" Now she displays a caring voice.

"Yeah, I'll fill you in lata."

"Well ok," she says, uneasy about the whole situation.

He rubs his eyes, starts pinching himself looking towards the bed. "Nope, not dreaming. It's real, she's here. Getting back in bed he buries his face in her neck. His dick grows hard poking her in her ass. She smiles, pushing back. He inserts his penis in her pussy, making deep love to her, showing her how much he missed her. After he busts 2 morning nuts, he spoons her, holding on tightly.

"Shawn, I'm so sorry, I'm so sorry. I was so mad my head was so fucked up I thought I hated you. I wanted revenge but since we been apart I know I love you. I don't want nobody but you Shawn please," she cries out, beggin'.

He places his finger over her mouth, licks her tears.

"I know. If I was you I would've did the same thing. I should've killed Jazz right away. I'm so loyal bae I couldn't see past him taking a bullet for me back when. I been thinking what would I do if I saw you again. Now I know, you can't help who you love. You tried to kill me but I still love you. I haven't had another woman since you been gone. I built myself back up. I thought about you the whole time. I love you. Now I really know now I do."

"I love you too, Shawn. Do you think we can work through all this?" She's being real.

"Is this what you want? 'Cause you been spending my bread like water. You know I know all the Island houses you bought. You was shopping at men's stores. I don't wanna know his name. I could've stopped the cards but I thought about it. All the shit I did ta ya for real I was like she'll be back one day and if she spends too much I'll stop that shit. It's your money too on the real."

"Shawn, you one in a million."

"Not really. Only for you," he tells her.

"Blair?"

"Yes?"

"I do have some loose ends I gotta take care of."

She turns, meeting him in his eyes.

"I never fucked her but we are growing close and shit."

Blair's face frowns but she can't get mad 'cause she been doing her thing. If Kurt wouldn't have left her, she would be still wit'em.

"Who is she? Do I know'a?"

"Nah, let me handle this one."

She smirks. "Alright. I'll give you that. Can we eat, then play nurse and doctor?"

"You know it," he says.

They start kissing again, re-uniting the flames that once burned within.

Chapter 27

"I can't believe I'm letting Blair play me like dis. I'm the one dat be doing all the playin'. I can't do dis shit ta Sasha. What about her mother? She was so good ta me. If it wasn't for them folks I wouldn't be where I am now physically. I love Blair. Why after all she did ta me, why I still love'a dough?" Shawn voices out loud, playing it out over many times in his head.

Honk. Honk. He blows his horn, pulling up to his man house.

Godey B looks out his screen door, squinting his eyes. Shawn lets down the window of his Escalade.

"Yo, nucca, it's me."

"Hell yeah!" his old commander and chief of his crew yells out. Godey B runs out his house holding his pants up around his waist. He runs around to the driver's side of the truck. "Mane, where you been Mane?" he questions, giving his boss some dap.

"Man, it's been real. It'a take like days ta even go over half dat shit kno'imean."

"I got weeks fo' ya, nucca. You comin' in? Sandy at work and shit," he makes mention, wanting to play catch up.

"I guess. I got a couple clicks ta spare." Shawn turns his truck off, then follows Godey B in his house that's located out in the boonies of Seven Locks, Maryland.

"Man, I can't believe all the shit you do. Yo ass still out here by the jailhouse, nucca. Ain't no way." Shawn shakes his head.

"20/20 is hindsight." As they approach the door, Godey B does what's natural—he opens the door for his old boss. "Make yourself comfortable. You drinking or I'm drinking alone?"

"Nah man, I stopped," Shawn enlightens him, taking a seat on the leather sofa.

"I ain't stop, so hold on," Godey B chirps, making his way to his stash. He returns wit' a bottle of Grey Goose. Sitting it on the table that separates them, "Ok talk to a brotha. What's been jumpin'?"

Shawn leans back, placing his forearm on the arm of the sofa with his hand resting on the side of his handsome face. "I'on know where ta start. It's been so much, mane."

"Start wit' you, nucca. Keep shit up front. You know how we do, we keep shit real." Godey comes raw.

"That's correct. You always keep shit real for sho," Shawn bounces back.

"Too old for anything else, got me?" Godey B adds.

"How old are you now, nucca?" Shawn laughs.

"Hell, how old am I? I think 45. Naw, let me see now … I'm 46. Hell, when you get my age you stop countin'." They continue to laugh. "What it be dough, mane. Stop stallin'." He takes a swig of that Goose sitting in front of him.

"Man, I'm fucked up. I love my wife, Blair, but I'm ... in love wit' this shawdy. She's an older lady named Sasha. I got fucked up sick. Sasha brought a nucca back ta life. Oh, she's a doctor, neurologist and shit. Her mother loves me. She's a physical therapist. I don't' know man. When I'm wit' shawdy we have fun. I'm relaxed, my guard down, but my hamma joint won't get up fo' shit wit'a."

"Hold up. I need ta take another swig on dat there shit. *Whoo whew*, you sho you'on want a swig, man? This done got real serious. You might need it. You got my nerves jumpin', mane. Your Johnson won't getty up for the occasion. Dat shit is some'em serious. I would kill myself, fuck what you heard," Godey B spits, sitting at attention now that he realizes how much trouble his man is in. At least to him.

"You got jokes, nucca." Shawn smirks. "Naw G, it ain't dat. I just don't seem ta be raising for Sasha but … as soon as I saw Blair my shit jump like 20 feet."

"Hell it ain't nutten else ta be said. Blair's the one all day, 'er day," Godey B explains.

"Mane, it ain't about dat no more for me."

"Nucca, you on some trippin' shit right now. What else could it possibly be about?" Godey's lost.

"What I'm getting ready to lace yo ears wit' don't go getting all wound up. Dis here shit 'bout my private shit. I came to you 'cause I trust you, number one. You older, done seen lots of shit. Number 2, you my main thoroughbred, feel that."

"Real talk, my nucca, now shoot." Godey B puts on his serious face, sitting back in his chair.

"Blair tried ta kill a nigga."

"What?! She did what?! Why dough?"

"Remember the night at the party when Jazz showed me the gang show of her?"

"Yeah, go ahead."

"Jazz told me she was active on it, then later he told me he put Ruffies in her drink."

"And?"

"And I didn't act on it. Man I didn't off dat nigga. He raped my wife. He lied to me. I made her look bad. Even though it happened before I met her or we started datin'. I was supposed ta handle dat shit, mane. I wasn't there for'a at her lowest point. She came face ta face wit' her rapist and my dumb ass didn't do shit but punk her out. I would've killed me too if I was her," he tells him, holding his head down moving it side to side. "Mane, I feel like a whole Bitch. I know I should've off'a. But I can't. I just can't, I love'a. I gotta admit the shit is so real. Me—the big tyma bossed up nigga. I offed niggas for less and I can't off her for trying to kill my ass," he adds, wiping the long tear that escapes his eye.

"You finished wit' that pity party shit?" Godey B shows no love, it seems.

Shawn raises his head, looking at'em like what you talking 'bout. Godey B sits up, leaning Shawn's direction, resting his arm on the chair's arm.

"Mane, you living life. Shit happens. You ain't exempt ta shit, nucca. The fucked up part about dis here is you didn't follow through as a real man should've. Dat shit that happened to your wife didn't have shit ta do wit' you. Dat shit happened before y'all started. Now yo boy, yeah you should've offed dat punk ass bitch right then and there no madda. Yeah, he took a bullet for you, granted, but dat shit didn't have shit ta do wit the situation that was at hand. I hated his punk ass anyway. But that's another story. He lied ta you point blank. Did she have the right ta fuck you up because of it? Hell yeah. You didn't show loyalty, and I fo one know that shit bleeds yo blood. She had the right ta make you suffer, so chalk that shit up. That's what women do. Hell has no fury like a woman scorned. Nucca, charge

dat shit ta the game. Here's the thing dough, you got a heart involved that's innocent that brought you back to life, back to me the crew. You owe her, hell yeah. But do you owe her at the expense of yo own happiness? That's some'em you my brotha gotta answer, 'cause it sounds like if yo wife catch you fuckin up it ain't gon' be a next time. Then I'ma have ta off her ass. Get yo life right, mane, 'cause you only have one."

Shawn gives his boy the look of why I come over here.

Knowing what he's thinking, "Mane, you came to see me 'cause you wanted the low down truth. Mane, my father always said in life we got choices. So I tell you *in life we got choices*. Choose wisely. Now can we go get some grub? 'Cause dis mushy shit making a mouse like me hungry."

"I love you, man," Shawn lets out.

"Nucca, you know I care. I'm just glad you a'ight. We gotta set some'em in place so we'll know when shit ain't right. You so private mane that shit gotta stop. Suppose you would have died? I wouldn't even be able to put you in the dirt."

"You right, man. You right."

"Let me get dressed so we can bounce," Godey B says, lifting from his chair.

Chapter 28

"Sasha, I'm so glad my son brought you over to meet me. It's been so long since I've been out anywhere with someone that doesn't have mental issues."

"These days you never know, right?" Sasha shoots, smiling.

"You right about that. What you going to order?" Shawn's mother asks.

"I think mac and cheese, ham."

"Umm, now that sounds good to me. I think I'll have the same."

They put in their orders, then make small talk while eating.

"That water looks nice. You wanna go for a walk along the bay?" Sasha asks.

"I would love to."

They pay for the food then exit the restaurant, take off their shoes, they walk along the bay digging their feet in the sand.

"Sasha, how is Shawndale doing? How is he making it through life?" his mother quizzes.

"He's doing fine, I guess. I haven't seen him in a week now." Sasha's voice cracks.

"One week, why? What's going on? You two having problems?"

"I'm not sure. He doesn't answer my calls."

"Have you been over to see him?"

"I went to his house. I kinda was spying though. I saw him come out so I called him. He looked at his phone then put it back in his pocket."

"Umph, you're a nice girl. Is he going through something?"

"Not that I know of," Sasha informs her.

"You know he doesn't tell me much about his life as I told you. He's never brought a woman to meet me. I know he must like you. He trusted you enough to let you into his deep dark world."

"Don't say that. You're not his dark world. He just loves you. He wants to protect you, that's all. Why would you think something like that?"

"Sasha, I have a mental illness. His father was killed by his stepmother. She was beautiful. She looks sorda like you. His father used to beat on women. I left. I got outta there. Needless to say he treated Shawndale well. He spoiled him rotten. I tried to take Shawn with me, but his father had the money, he had the power. My family had money, just as much, but they weren't willing to help because I was sick. They felt it was best that Shawn be raised by his father Copeland.

"I didn't get to see Shawndale until he was 12. Thanks to his stepmother Annie, she brought him to the hospital to visit me once a week. She never told Copeland. When Shawndale slipped up one day and told Copeland he like to killed that poor woman, may she rest in peace. I never understood why she didn't get out. When Shawn was older he told his father he was going to visit me. He went off on Shawndale, started beating on him with the butt of his gun like he was a man on the streets that stole something from Shawndale. Annie grabbed the gun and shot Copeland to death right in from of Shawndale. One month later they found Annie dead. I know Shawndale killed her for killing Copeland. It was then he changed for the worse. He was in college, he dropped out, he started selling like his father. He hand no need. That's what I didn't understand. His father left him more money than the law would allow. Annie's insurance policy was every bit of 10 million alone. My mother and father left everything to Shawndale because of my illness. Copeland's father left everything to Shawn. He's a very rich man, my Shawndale. His money will never run out. My mother and father had bonds that are a lifetime so he gets money every month until he dies, then it will pass

on to his child. See, Sasha, his mind is messed up too but in a different way. If you love my son, *fight*. Don't give up unless he's beating on you or verbally abusing you. What I'm saying is sometimes you have to sweep things under the rug to survive a lifetime of love."

Sasha stops in her tracks, facing her. "Thanks, Mrs. Hope. I needed to hear this."

"You're welcome. Now is it anything else you want to talk about?' Mary says.

"Yes, I went to the store yesterday …"

They continue to talk and walk. Sasha has so much love for his mother.

Chapter 29

Blair has been loving her old life. Shawn does so much for her. They go out a lot, make beautiful love, party, have fun. She's so happy Shawn understood why she did what she did. He assures her that the past is in the past. They decide they will never speak of it again. Blair told Shawn she wants to come off birth control. He was shocked but happy at the same time. She can't believe what she did to him. She made a bigger mistake by sleeping with his so-called friend, Kurt. She calls him on his cell.

"Wuss up?" Kurt addresses her.

"You. What you up to?" Blair sings.

"Shit, what you up to?"

"Nutten. I was thinking maybe we can meet up for some drinks?" She puts it out there.

"And you know I can. What time?"

"Say 2."

"Two it is, bae." Kurt smiles, nothing but sex on the brain.

Blair reaches TGI Friday fifteen minutes early, gets a table, orders their drinks.

Two minutes later Kurt shows up.

"Hey you," she greets with a cheese ball smile. He hugs and kisses her on the cheek.

"Hey sexy." He takes his seat. "Why you got on all that shit? You'on need contacts, what up wit' that green wig? Really? You lunching, just be you when you wit' me," he tells her.

"Change is good. Anyway, I already ordered your drinks. Top shelf scotch, no ice."

"You remembered I like that."

"Sure I did. How could I forget? You used to pour it on me, then suck it off."

"No doubt," he grins.

When their food is served they eat and talk.

"I miss you, Kurt."

"Miss you too. We had so much fun."

She tells him as he downs his drink, "You want another?" she asks.

"Might as well, since it's gon' be a long night here you tell it."

"So you remember them long sex sections?" She piggybacks off his thoughts.

"*Um whoo* what's in this drink?" He bends forward, holding his head. "I need some water. I'm sweating like a mug."

Kurt tries to stand. "Oh shit, shawdy, shit. My head is dizzy."

"Kurt, you ok!" Blair lifts up.

"I'on know."

He falls to the floor.

"Sir, you alright?" a customer sitting behind them asks.

"Get help!" Blair shouts.

"My body is cold, Blair … Blai—I—B—"

Blair bends over, pressing her warm lips to his ear, "You played me. You took me for a ride. This is what happens when you fuck over women, you no good muthafucka. You took my pussy, my husband's money, my love. If I can't have you then nobody can. Now you die in peace. I'll send your baby momma to be with you soon, don't worry."

Kurt looks at Blair, shocked. He can't speak. His body is getting colder. She runs her hand over his eyelids, closing them, sending him to meet the angels.

Chapter 30

"Sasha, I'm sorry I've been so busy," Shawn says through the phone. "I just haven't had the time."

"I understand," she lies. "Shawn, tell me what's going on with you. Why are you avoiding me for real? I'm a big girl," she assures him, as she drives in her car.

"What you mean?" He plays dumb.

She goes the extra mile tonight. She drives to his house, knocks on his door. He rushes to the door, opens it, sees her. He grabs her by her arms, marches her to the panic room as fast as he can before Blair comes home.

"What's wrong? Why you drag on me like that?"

"What you doing here?!"

She opens her fur coat—nothing but skin.

He licks his chops, telling her, "Damn you look good."

"How you going to respond to all this?" she asks, winding her hips in a circular motion.

This time his dick is at attention. Taking his pants off, she falls to her knees taking all of him in her mouth.

When he is fully hard she takes him by his hand, leading him to the room. She lies her sexy body on the bed. Shawn climbs in-between her legs, pressing his 9-inch manhood inside her. In 10 minutes he nuts. Not wanting her to know it was quick for him, he keeps going, nuttin' over and over. Sasha moans softly. His hands caress her soft skin. When he gets his last good nut he takes his soft penis out, raises up.

"Oh shit you bleedin', Sasha. Did I hurt you?"

She shakes her head no.

It's then he relaxes. She's a virgin he figures out.

"I was your first?"

She nods.

"But you 40, fuck." He puts his hands over his head, lying on his back.

"I'm sorry," she voices, feeling small about now.

"No, it's not that."

"Did I do something wrong?" she asks.

He snickers. "No, nothing. It was all good, all good. Sasha, shit is complicated right now."

"What you mean complicated?" She's lost.

"I'm back wit' my wife."

"You're what?!" She jumps up, grabs her long length fur.

"How could you?! She tried to kill you!"

"It's complicated. I love her but I'm in love wit' you. Please try and understand."

"So that's why you stopped taking my calls. That's why you stopped talking to me. Did she come back here?"

"Yeah."

"I gotta go. I gotta get some air."

He grabs her by her arm. "Sasha, I'ma make dis right I promise."

Her eyes start shining, holding back the tears. She loves Shawn dearly.

"I'm sorry, Shawn. I can't play second fiddle for no one."

So she runs off.

"Fuck!" Shawn yells.

Chapter 31

Sasha speeds down Waterfront line. Jamming on brakes, she throws her car in park, turns off her engine, rushes up the walkway. She lets herself in Mary's house.

"Ma, Mary!"

"Yes baby yes?" Mary runs to the front of her house from the garden with her garden gloves still on. "What's the matter, child. Talk to me. What is it?'

"It's Shawn. He's back with her!"

"Back with who? Calm your nerves, child. You want some of my lemonade?'

"No, I want him. I want Shawn."

"Ok, ok wait here," Mary says, going to the kitchen pouring some good old fashion lemonade anyway. She hands it off to Sasha.

Mary takes a seat beside her at the table.

Sasha takes a sip of the lemonade.

"That's good. It seems to help calm me some. Thank you."

"Glad it can help you. Now tell me what's wrong, my sweetness."

"It's Shawn. He told me he's back with his wife."

"His what? What wife are you talking about, baby?"

"His wife."

"Shawn's married? My Shawn?" His mother is baffled,

"Yes, she tried to kill him," Sasha says.

Mary begs her to tell her the story in its entirety. Sasha obliges. Once she's done, "My Lord. My God, was this in the Fort Washington house?" his mother asks.

"Yes."

"Is he still there now?"

"Yes, yes, yes!" she wails louder.

"Oh my Jesus please, please protect my child," she lets out, moving about reaching for some napkins, handing them to Sasha.

Sasha blows her nose. "I'm sorry. It just hurts, you know."

"I know. I'm just wondering why he would bring you to meet me then do something like this. It just doesn't make sense. You don't worry. I'll handle this."

Sasha stops crying. "You can't tell him. He'll hate me for telling you."

"I would never tell him anything like that, don't you worry. I fried some snappers. Would you like some? You need to eat."

"I'm not hungry."

"You have got to eat, baby."

"If you insist."

Mary walked to the kitchen. Sasha turns her head smiling like she just won round one.

Chapter 32

"This is Blair. Hey you, what you up to?" Blair asks her homegirl Rena over the phone.

"Nutten, girl. Just home working, that's all."

"Working?"

"Working on this masters. Speaking of which, when you going back and finishing school?"

"Neva. What I need to do that for, all this money we got?"

"I guess you right. I'm glad you found one another again."

"Me too. I was miserable for real."

"I know. I was hearing it in your voice," Rena tells her.

"Bae!" Shawn walks through the door yelling.

"In here," Blair spits.

"Rena, speaking of the devil he appears." They laugh.

"I hear you. Call me when you can. Bye."

"Bye." Blair ends the call. "Hello, baby," she greets, wearing her bootie shorts and a cutoff top, sitting on their king size canopy bed that has a mirror built in the top of it.

"Baby, Kurt dead."

"Kurt? Who is Kurt?" She plays it off.

"You know, my man from the A," he reminds her.

"Nope, don't remember him."

"Anyway he's dead, man. They say he was on a date and died in TGI Fridays. Damn, that was my boy. I'ma have to send his fam some money. All them kids, his wife … man, Simone too. She was a sweetheart."

"Was she the one wit' him when he died?" Blair asks.

"The police don't seem to know. They say they didn't even get her info. That's how good they did their fuckin job. You know how that goes. He's a nigga. What they care, right?"

"I feel you on that, bae. Either way it's fucked up."

"Maybe it's for the best 'cause his wife don't need all that drama. I'm hoping she was a fly-by-night, you know."

"If you say so."

"So who is Simone?"

"She one of his baby mommas. He got a wife he live wit', then Simone. He loves her but then again he got like two other children by some random chicks. That nigga used ta use broads left and right."

"I see," she responds, boiling on the inside.

"The thing is Simone she don't be caring who he was wit'. She knew his Gigolo games. Her motto was as long as he brought back the money, she didn't care."

"Wow, that's messed up. Where she live? Maybe we can go now. I know she needs somebody that she can relate to," Blair says.

"She stay in Oxon Hill. His wife in Potomac."

That was *his wife I saw, huh?* she's thinking.

"His wife had her face done over. She took a bullet for that fool. She used ta be fine but after that bullet … man, not so much now."

"You funny, stop it. I'm sure she'on look that bad, Shawn." She smiles.

"Bae, let's just say she couldn't bring me mail." They laugh. She throws a pillow at him. He ducks. "I'm being real dough."

"You coming wit' me to see his fam?"

She hesitates, taking him in.

"What? What's wrong?" he asks, returning her gaze.

"I love you so much," she tells him, getting off the bed. She walks up to him. "Can I get served first?"

"I thought you'd neva ask."

Chapter 33

"Hello, when I'ma see you again?" Sasha asks through the phone.

"How about tomorrow night?" Shawn answers.

"I have to work at the hospital. How about tonight?"

"I can't do it tonight. I got other plans. My man died. I'm going to visit the fam in a minute, as a matter of fact."

"I'm sorry to hear that. Who you going with?"

"C'mon, Sash. That's not for us."

"You're right. Make time for me when you can."

"That's my girl," he tells her, hoping she really gets it. "I'll talk to you lata," he adds.

"Ok, bye."

"Don't say it like that," he orders her.

"What you want me to say?"

"Nutten, I'll call you lata."

She ends the call, waiting up the road from his house. Thirty minutes pass. She sees him and Blair in his truck

pulling out his driveway. She drives into the driveway, gets out, sticks her old key in the lock. She enters, going straight to the master bedroom. She goes to Blair's closet first, smelling her clothes, looking at her lipsticks, admiring her tastes in stuff. Then she goes to his belongings; by the same token she does his stuff the same way. After she's done, she lays in their bed, smelling the pillow.

"No pictures," she whimpers to herself.

After an hour she leaves. As she drives down the road, *Shawn you'll be all mines. I will fight for what is mines.*

Her cell breaks her thoughts.

"Hello?"

"Hey, Sash, it's me Blair. What you doing?"

"Hi, Blair. I'm doing nothing. I have a call at the hospital. After that, nothing."

"Good. Meet me at the Ruby Tuesday's."

"What time?

"9 or 10. Whatever is good for you."

"How about 9? If that's good for you. I'm like an old person. The earlier, the better. Is it ok if Cody joins us?"

"Sure, why not."

"Blair, I needed this."

"Me too, girl."

"See you later then."

"At nine, don't forget," Blair repeats, walking up to Simone's door behind Shawn.

"I won't."

Additionally, Sasha calls Cody and confirms that she can make it too.

Chapter 34

"Over here, Cody." Blair waves.

"Howdy, where's Sasha?" is the first thing Cody asks.

"Late."

"That's not like her."

"She said she had a hospital run first, and that she might be running a little late," Blair explains. "We can order drinks until she comes."

"Sounds good to me." Cody goes along wit' the idea.

They sit, order drinks, make good convo about the streets.

"Hi, you guys sorry I'm late. Had a patient. Bills must get paid, right?" Sasha rolls up yawing.

"I was starting to die from starvation," Cody pouts.

They all order their meals, japing it up.

"Blair, you seem so happy. Last time we talked you said you got your old man back. What even happened to the other one? The one you traveled with a lot?" Sasha asks, cutting into her chicken.

"Girl, you know how that goes." Blair plays it off.

"No, Blair, she don't. She's a 40-year-old virgin," Cody clowns.

"Better than being a 40-year-old whore."

"I knew you was glowing," Cody remarks.

Blair laughs.

Sasha ignores the dry joke.

"Sash, she was just joking. I thought it was funny. Tell us about your patient," Blair adds.

"No, not tonight. You tell me what has got you ringing," Sasha says, pointing out the ring that's flashing on her ring finger.

"Yes, I must confess. I got back with my husband."

"I thought the travel man was your husband," Sasha says, cutting her eye Cody's way.

"I called him that 'cause we were playing house but I have a true husband who I needed to give another chance."

"Who is this husband?" Cody asks.

"For starters, he's handsome, delicate, we went through a lot of problems in the past 'cause of communication. But needless to say we getting it together. Shit not gon' happen overnight but it's one thing we know and that is we love one another. We have too much to let it go so easy, you know?"

"I hear that. Isn't love great when it's with the right man?"

"Yes, and my Shawn—"

Sasha hears Shawn's name and starts gagging, spitting her food everywhere.

"You ok?!" Blair asks.

Cody jumps out her seat.

"You need water?! Are you ok?!" she asks, beating her in the back.

"Yeah, something just went down the wrong pipe, maybe a pepper," Sasha says with a choked throat, grabbing her water. "Don't stop, tell me more. I love to hear about my friend's love stories," she adds, eyes all watery.

"Yeah, tell us more," Cody follows. Cody looks at her friend knowing her man's name is Shawn too.

"Are you sure you're gonna be ok?" Blair asks, concerned about her newfound friend.

"I'm good. I think a pepper went down the wrong pipe, that's all," Sasha lies, taking in another sip of cold water.

"As I was saying his name is Shawn. I left him for a small minute then I came back. We're fine now. Such is life, you know?"

"Where do you two live?" Cody asks.

"Excuse me. I think I need the restroom." Sasha races off to the restroom, throwing up everything in her stomach. Flushing the toilet she makes an about face.

"*Whew*, Cody, you scared me."

"What you gon' do? That's her husband," Cody lets out.

"I know now. I'm going to release him. I can't be with her husband. I consider her my friend now."

"A crazy friend for Christ's sake. She tried to kill'em."

"I know that too. Look, Cody, let me handle this. I'm a big girl. I'm ok. And how do we know the whole story? He is back with her, you see."

"You have a point there. Let's get back before she grows suspicious. You know he's making a mistake. She's not nowhere as pretty as you."

"Looks aren't everything, you know."

"No, I don't know."

Sasha washes her hands, then the both of them exit the restroom making their way back to Blair.

Chapter 35

Three Days Pass

Knock. Knock. Blair knocks lightly.

"Yes coming, hold on."

"Well hello you," says Blair after Simone opens the door. "Do you remember me? My husband and I came over to see you when Kurt died."

"I remember. Come in, excuse the place. I haven't had time to clean up. You know how that goes."

"No problem. Did they ever find the cause of death?" Blair asks Simone.

"They say insulin. I couldn't believe that. He never said anything about him being diabetic, least I don't remember. They closed the case before I could say anything. You know it was up to his wife. She just told them not to go any further with the case. She just wanted to bury him. She said she was tired. Can you believe that shit?! *Tired.*"

"Did they retrieve the cameras from TGI Fridays?" Blair has to know.

"No, they say he was with a blond with light gray eyes, light complexion, driving a Chevy Truck. They say she gave her statement. The other customers agreed with her statement and that was that."

"Wow! What kind of investigation was that?"

"My point exactly. Plus the cameras were broke," she informs Blair, who is happy to hear that.

"I hope this will help. I made some pie. It's so good. It's not for kids, though." Putting her finger up to her mouth in a *shh* motion, "It has a little something in it to calm you, if you know what I mean."

"Girl, you know I need that."

"Well I just wanted to stop by again to say hello and check on you. I know how it is to lose someone you love. I'll check in on you again. Maybe next time you and I can go out, do some shopping or something like that," Blair tells her.

"Thanks, you're so nice. Thanks for stopping by as well."

"No problem." Blair makes her exit. "You enjoy every drop of the pie."

"I know I will," she says, closing her door.

Blair gets in her car. Sitting behind her steering wheel, "One down, one more to go. I knew they would find the insulin in his body. Oh well, he deserved it. Ole foul ass nut bastard pig. And Sasha you think I'm stupid. I know you

fucking Shawn. How y'all met, I don't know but it will end, believe that. You said you was choking on a pepper but you didn't have peppers in your food. You slipped. We ordered the same damn thing. I guess those law classes really work, huh?

Chapter 36

"Baby, can you believe they found Simone dead? That shit creepy, right?" Shawn pronounces while standing over Blair as she sits on the couch watching ratchet TV.

"I know. She bled to death. I heard you on the phone just now."

"Yeah, that shit crazy. Maybe she had high blood or some'em." Shawn tries to make sense of it all.

"Maybe," Blair utters, thinking about the bottle of blood thinner she put in the apple pie she handed her that day.

"Man, life is some'em. One day you alive, the next you dead. This shit is crazy, real crazy." He continues to talk about it in disbelief.

Blair eyeballs him when the commercial comes on. "Baby, your cell is lightin' up."

"Let it ring. Ain't shit going on that I need to get to when I'm spending time wit' you, right?"

"Answer it. It might be important. The last call was about that lady, so who knows." She looks at him with innocent eyes.

He pulls his mobile off his hip. "Hello?"

"Hi, it's me. What you doing?"

"Yoo," he says, not wanting Blair to know who it is.

"I just wanted to tell you I'm pregnant."

"Ok, meet me in 30 minutes at our spot."

"She right there?" Sasha asks.

"You got it."

"Ok, you mean my house."

"Fo' sho."

"Ok, I'll be here," Sasha tells him.

"I'll be ok, I got you," he lets out.

"I know. See you in 30 minutes."

"Baby, some'em did come up. I'ma have ta make a move."

"It's Sasha, ain't it?"

He draws his head back. "Who?"

"Sasha," she says casually.

"Who is Sasha?"

Maybe they not messing around, she thinks to herself before answering, "Nobody, I'm trippin'." *I know he's telling the truth 'cause he did say who in the hell is Sasha. He didn't get mad,* she thinks to herself.

"Blair, don't start that crazy shit. I can't do it. Not this time around. I'm not wit' nobody but you. That girl I was telling you about, we broke it off. I told her er'thing. She's good. She was hurt but we didn't do shit so it wasn't hard work."

"I'm sorry. You right. I'll wait here. I gotta let my wall down."

"You do 'cause we starting over, right?" He looks her in the eye with a serious face.

She nods yes.

"Good," he says, pecking her on her lovely lips. "I'll see you in a minute. Maybe we can go catch a movie and grab a bite ta eat."

Her face softens. "That sounds good. Drive careful."

"You know it," he assures her, standing, reaching for his keys, heading out the door.

"I guess I was wrong about Sasha after all. She gets to live … for now."

Chapter 37

Ding ding! Ding ding! Ding!

"Ok, stop ringing the damn bell. I'm coming!" Blair hollers through the door.

"It's me, open up."

Blair opens the front door, standing in her robe.

"Why you ringin' my gotdamn bell like that?"

"Your bell? No, my dear, it's my bell. Where is my son?" Mary stands in the doorway holding her bags, staking claim.

Blair jerks her head back. "Your what?!"

"You heard me. You must be the wife I never met."

"Lady, you trippin'. I think you have the wrong house."

"Blair, bae, who's at the door?" Shawn walks up.

"Some lady claiming to be your mother."

"My who?" he says, reaching the door, "Ma!" he lets out like he's staring at a ghost.

"Yes, it's me. I can't visit my son?"

"I got this, bae," Shawn says, moving in front of Blair.

"Are you going to let me in my own house?"

"My bad, sure." He moves to the side, allowing her entry.

She steps in, bags in tow. She cases the place. Blair gapes. She's intimidated. She speaks, walking on her husband's heels, "You told me your mother was dead."

"She is," Mary and Shawn say in unison.

Shawn explains, "My stepmother, the lady that raised me, is dead. This is my real mother, Mary. Ma, this is Blair."

"Hello, Blair."

"Hello, nice to meet you. Sorry I didn't know who you were." Blair sticks her hand out for a truce.

Mary looks at it. She starts walking around, visiting room after room.

"Shawn, the house—amazingly—still looks the same."

"Yap, I didn't change nutten. Dad's room is still where it was. All his stuff still in place."

"Oomph." She curves her lips. "How about the room he kept me in for years?"

"It's still there. I just added some gym stuff, that's all. You wanna go see it?"

She looks at him, rolling her eyes as if to say no you didn't ask me that.

She stops at the kitchen, glancing over at Blair.

"Can you cook?"

Blair looks at Shawn, who hunches his shoulders. "Yes."

"I'm hungry. How about you?" his mother voices.

"What you like?" Blair asks.

"No, the question is what *you* like?" she shoots back at'a.

"Everything."

"So did you all eat yet?"

"No, ma'am," Blair tells her.

"Good."

"Ma, how long you staying?" Shawn voices.

"As long as I want to. It's my house, ain't it?"

"True dat."

"How you been, son?"

"Fine."

"Your eyes say different."

"I'm good, Ma."

"Are you going to take my bags to the guest room while I get started cooking?"

He wraps his hands around her bags.

"Blair, you come with me so we can do girl talk."

Blair eyeballs Shawn, who gives her his blessing.

"Ma, I was leaving," Shawn says. "I'ma holla at y'all later."

Blair gives him the look of death. He smiles like shit funny.

Chapter 38

Shawn's mother is still at the house. She cooks, clean, shops, keeping low, allowing Shawn and Blair to do them.

Mary hangs out a lot with Sasha and her mother; she's grown to love them both. She's so happy about her first grandchild in which Shawn now knows is his. They had a DNA test done. Sasha wasn't too happy about that at all. He told her he will support the child but the child couldn't come to his house just yet. Blair knows nothing about the child.

Sasha avoids Blair at all costs these days. She stopped answering her calls. Blair got the hint and stopped calling altogether, thinking Sasha thinks she's just too good for her. Shawn's mother doesn't like it, the way he treats Sasha. She minds her business though. She told Shawn he will not keep her away from the baby or Sasha's family. Shawn told her to do whatever she wants, but he gotta do him his way.

Mary and Blair lounge in the solarium at the house. Mary is knitting; Blair is doing a crossword puzzle.

"Ma Mary, do you know who the group was that sung 'Fire'?"

"Why yes, Chile. You young people, that was real music. Not like this stuff you all listen to today. It was The Ohio Players."

"Oh good, it fits too," she says, writing it in her crossword.

"Blair, would you like some good old lemonade?"

"How can I turn down your lemonade?" Blair says, sitting back in her chair.

"Good. I want some too." Mary lifts up, moving to the kitchen. "When did Shawndale say he would be home?"

"Tomorrow. He had to go up to New York for something," Blair tells her.

"This New York business he opened for us is taking so much of his time," Mary says while making the lemonade.

"I know. All this money we have and he wants to open a company, talking 'bout it's a good thing to do something with our time. But it looks like he doing all the something. It's ok, it gives him something to do. Gives me reason to miss him," Blair spits.

Mary walks back to the solarium, lemonade and cups in hand. Sitting it on the stand, she pours them some, handing Blair hers. She takes a seat, holding her cup in the air.

"Here's to New York."

"To New York," Blair says. They tap cup to cup, then Blair gulps her drink down. "That was cold and good."

"I see you drank that down. You were thirsty, wasn't you? Would you like more?" Mary asks.

"I'm good. I think I'ma take a nap."

"You go do that. It's a good day for it, all this rain."

"Call me if you need me or if Shawn calls."

"I will. You get some rest, child."

Blair makes her way to the bed, taking off her slides. She lies her head on her pillow.

"What she put in that drink? My head is so heavy. Shawn, is that you?" she asks, unable to lift her head. It's just so heavy.

"It's me."

"I thought you was coming back tomorrow?" she says, slurring.

"I was but I couldn't miss seeing you die."

"What?!" Blair tries to lift her head but she can't. "What was in the drink—?" Her words start to fall off.

"It don't madda for where you going."

"Wh ... why ...?" she makes out.

Mary joins him. "Now you rest. I told you you would love my lemonade, didn't I?" She puts her arm around her son's waist.

"Did you think you was gon' get away with trying to kill me, bitch?" Shawn seethes. "Didn't yo mother tell you about an Eye for a fuckin Eye."

"But … why?" She tries to talk. She puts her hands towards him but they're too heavy to lift. She feels her throat swelling. She's losing air. Her eyelids become heavier. They close as she breathes out her last breath of life.

Epilogue

After that night Shawn and his mother never spoke about it again. Shawn buried Blair in style. He told her family she died of some drug she was on that he knew nothing about. He waited seven months before marrying Sasha, gave her the same spiel as he gave Blair's family—not that she cared. Sasha had thought of killing her as well.

Shawn and Sasha had a beautiful little girl. They named her Shawness. Shawn's mother hates that name. She says the little girl needs her own identity. Shawn said that's why they put "ness" on the end of her name. His mother just laughed as she packed her bags to head back to Chesapeake.

"Shawn, come on. Shawness is ready. We're going to be late for her ballet recital."

"I'm coming, baby." Shawn makes it down the steps. He pauses, his eyes roll up and down, observing his family standing by the door. *I couldn't have made a better choice.* "Let's go, y'all. Oh wait, let me take a picture of you and my princess. "

Pulling out his iPhone, he snaps the photo, sends a copy to his mother.

"I love you so much, baby. I can never imagine life without you and my baby girl," he expresses to her.

"I know you do. And I have to tell you I'm aware of what you did to make it possible for us to be together as a family," she spits.

"What you talking about?"

"Blair. I'm not dumb, you know. But your secret is safe with me. I want you to know I think that's real love what you did. She deserved it after what she did to you."

"I have no idea what you talkin' 'bout. All I know is I love you and we gon' be late."

"Shawn, you're the best father and husband a woman can have. I'm your ride or die woman, believe this," she says with a smile, holding their daughter in her arms.

Shawn smiles. "That's why you standing here now."

Sasha takes a look around her new mansion located in Tysons, Virginia. *I love my life,* she thinks to herself as she walks into the sunny outdoors.

Shawn opens the back car door for Sasha, puts the baby in the car seat then he opens the car door for her to get in. After she's in he walks in front of the car, letting himself in, starts the car, looks over at his beautiful woman, puts the car in gear, pulls out the drive way—

BAM!

The airbags of his Benz deploy, jerking his body back and her neck. He thought he heard Sasha's neck snap but he's not sure. Reaching over, he grabs her.

"BABY, YOU OK! SASHA SPEAK, PLEASE!"

Coming to his senses he looks back at the baby who is looking at him.

"Good, you ok."

Turning his head back to Sasha, he sees blood oozing out her nose. He panics, trying to get past the air bags. He pulls her body close to him. He tries pushing on her door but it's jammed. He sees fire out the corner of his eye. Looking up he now sees it's the hood of his car—it's on fire!

Looking back at his daughter he pulls her out her seat, holding her in one hand. He continues to try and save Sasha, whose body is limp. He gets out the car.

"RENA, WHAT THE FUCK?!" he yells, still holding his daughter.

She looks at him, then the car, stepping back. She watches the flames as they grow bigger.

"I know you killed her!" Rena screams at Shawn. "She came to me in my dream. You did it. You and your mother, you son of a bitch!"

"You did this shit 'cause of that?" he spits fire.

"Hell yeah. You killed my best friend, my sister, so I killed yo bitch, nigga!"

He tries to rush her but she's too quick. In all of that he forgot about his wife. When he remembers he makes an about face, but it's too late—the flames have taken over the entire car.

"*Noooooooo!*" he screams at the top of his lungs.

Looking back at Rena he falls to his knees.

"Why why, she was all I had!"

"And Blair was all I had, you bitch! I thought you knew—hell has no fury like a woman scorned! And I'm one scorned bitch right now!"

The following is an UrbanSnapshot™, a stand-alone short story:
21 Days of Secrets *by J.J. Jackson:*

Day 1

Shit, I'm running late. My first temp job. Hell it seems like I can't do nothing right these days. If I miss this damn job how I'ma explain that to my P.O.? One more month and I'ma free fuckin woman, Gia thinks to herself as she brushes her teeth. When she's done, she walks into her closet and starts throwing stuff around looking for a pair of shoes to match her suit.

"This clean. Life is so hard for a bitch. Damn, I miss hacking them government computers. Shit was sweet. We made $50,000 a month. I was living on easy street until David got popped. Then his ass decided he wanted to play true confession. And they say women can't hold water. It had'ta been a man that made that lie up. But them was the good old days fo' sho. There you are, my pretty little shoes. I gotta do some'em 'bout this damn closet. 'Cause I know I just straightened this fucka up last week," she says out loud. She takes a look at herself in her mirror, making sure everything looks the part for her new job.

A bitch sho nuff look good. I thank God for Brittany. She gotta be the best booster on this side of the east coast. These Chanel shoes

and this three-piece Valentine pinstripe mini skirt suit is setting my sexy ass off. Damn it feels good to be me, Gia adds to her thoughts while slipping her $800 Chanel oversized shades on. She takes one last look.

"Now that's what a bitch talking 'bout. Dang, Gia, you fine," she compliments herself one last time.

Gia has always been a beautiful girl. She's never had any problems getting the man she wants. Well in that case nor has she had problems getting a woman either. Gia's measurement are 48D-23-36. She has long slender legs, a basketball ass, her hair is long, bone straight to be exact. Her skin is flawless, she has light grey eyes with a nice brown complexion as if she has a built-in tan. Her beauty will put any women to shame and she knows it, but it's one thing about Gia—her attitude stinks. If she can't have it then no one can. Gia has always used what God has given her to get whatever it is she wants.

She has no limits.

"Well, it's that time," she says then she leaves her apartment, hops in her convertible all black Mini Cooper, driving off to the sounds of Drake's, "Started From The Bottom."

She weaves in and out of traffic as she drives down Suitland Parkway. When she reaches downtown DC she pulls into the parking garage of her new job assignment located on 19th Street. She gets a ticket then parks her ride. She walks into the building.

"Hold, hold the elevator please!" she yells out, running towards the closing doors.

The young man on the elevator sticks his arm through the door so they won't close. Gia boards the elevator with folders in hand.

"Thank you, sir. I'm running late," she tells him, feeling like she's lost her wind. *A bitch gotta join a gym,* she thinks to herself.

"What floor?" the young man asks.

"Oh, um, shit what floor?" Gia repeats as she fumbles through some papers. She stops at a blue sticky.

"Eight, it's the eighth floor," she says, looking down at the number on the sticky.

"So you're going to Smith Fordham and Burt Accountant firm?" he raps.

"Yes, the largest in the world," she replies, looking him up and down, lowering her shades smiling.

They reach the 3rd floor. Another man boards.

"Hi, Ted," the man on the elevator greets.

"Hi, Bill."

Gia looks at Bill. *Oh my God he is fine as hell. I would serve him breakfast lunch and dinner all at the same time,* Gia is thinking to herself as she feels her kittie start to moisten. Gia drops her folders. Bill and Ted look down. She starts to bend over to pick them up.

"Oh no, let me," Bill says, reaching down to help Gia. Their eyes melt into one.

"What's your name, Gorgeous?" Bill asks her, handing her the folders.

"Giovanni, but everyone calls me Gia for short," she tells him, blushing.

Ding. The elevator sounds off as the doors open.

"Well, this our floor," Bill turns to Ted saying.

"Oh you two work on this floor?" Gia asks.

"Yes we do," the both of them answer in unison.

"Good morning, Mr. Smith," one of the workers greets as Bill enters the office.

"Good morning, Mr. Fordham," another says.

"Good morning, ladies," Bill replies as he looks back at Gia with a slight smirk on his handsome round face.

Gia's heart drops when she realizes she just rode up the elevator with two of the top executives of the largest AA firm in the world. Then she collects her thoughts. *This is gon' be a double blessing,* she's thinking as she walks over to the receptionist desk.

Day 2

"Hi, my name is Gia Shirley. I'm from Master's Temps," she tells the receptionist.

"You're the new temp. Have a seat over there and someone will be with you," the white young lady orders, pointing to the lobby area full of seats. Then she lowers her head, answering her switchboard as if to say you're dismissed.

"Bitch," Gia mumbles under her breath, turning and walking to the lobby area.

Gia takes a seat. She waits for one hour before an older lady shows up.

"You must be Mrs. Shirley?" the older lady says, holding out her hand for a shake.

"That would be me," Gia responds with a fake smile. She's pissed as hell that she had to wait one whole hour so she doesn't put her hand out for the friendly greet. The lady looks down at her hand. Noticing it's coming up empty, she drops it to her side.

"I'm sorry for the long wait but we had an unexpected board meeting."

"I understand," Gia lies.

"Well, Ms. Shirley, follow me. You'll be working here for 6 months as Mr. Smith's assistant. He's the lead partner of this company. His old assistant went to our office in New York to train for her new position. That makes this position open for hire," she informs Gia.

"Oh, really? That's a good thing for me," Gia tells her with excitement in her voice.

The lady eyeballs Gia, stopping in her tracks.

"Ms. Shirley, you're funny. We don't hire Temps." She tries to get Gia back for not shaking her hand. She's trying to belittle her by looking her up and down. But Gia being Gia thinks fast on her feet.

"Oh no, I didn't mean *I* wanted the job. I meant it's better for me that someone will be taking the position in about six months. Ms. ...?"

The lady finally tells Gia her name. "Oh, it's Mrs. Jones."

"Ok, Mrs. Jones. Because I'll be getting your job," Gia says, then they bust out into laughter.

"You're a very funny lady," Mrs. Jones lets on.

"Only if you knew you're going to be my first victim," Gia says under her breath.

"Ok, Gia, this is your desk right outside Mr. Smith's office. He will tell you what he wants. Now if you have too many mess ups I'll have to call Master Temps and have you replaced. Do I make myself clear?" Mrs. Jones tells her, looking over her glasses.

"Very clear. Tell me something, Mrs. Jones …"

"Anything."

"Did the temp agency tell you anything about me?"

"No. We just tell them what we want and they send the perfect person for the job every time. We've been dealing with this agency for 25 years so we trust them fully. Is there something we should know about you except that you're a walking label?"

Mrs. Jones strikes again, surveying Gia's gear.

"No. And for the record I'm a good worker who happens to love high fashion," Gia tells her, now scanning her inventory.

Non-dressing bitch, she can't afford my underwear, Gia is thinking.

"Mrs. Jones, what is it that you do here? If you don't mind me asking."

"I'm the head of control. That means—"

"I know what that means. You're the boss," Gia cuts into her sentence.

"Look here, you little—"

"And here comes Mr. Smith," Gia cuts her short again. "Hello again, Mr. Smith," Gia spits with a smile.

Mrs. Jones glances at him. "You two met?"

"Kind of," says Mr. Smith. "I do know I like her, Mrs. Jones. So make sure you treat her as one of the family. Who knows, I may just keep her on board. She seems bright and she's beautiful. We need someone fresh like flowers in this office. Wouldn't you agree?" he asks her, winking at Gia.

"I'll order them flowers right now, Sir," Gia says, picking up the phone feeding into Mr. Smith's sarcasm.

When Bill walks back into his office, "You need anything else?" Gia says with the phone to one ear, a smile on her cute little sneaky face.

"Don't fuck wit' me, young lady," Mrs. Jones lets out, heading down the hall.

"You ain't seen nutten yet. Gia's here, bitch. And I will be the HBIC real soon."

Day 3

"Gia, can you come in my office with your tablet?" Mr. Smith summons her.

"Yes, Sir," Gia says, grabbing her tablet, hurrying to impress her fine ass boss. She is wearing an all-white Ferragamo mini dress with some Tom Ford Croc pumps. She's dressed for sex.

"You rang?" Gia stands in front of his desk and asks.

He looks up. "Uh, um, umm ..." He has to clear his throat, loosen his collar so he can catch his breath.

Why does she have to be so young plus fine all at the same time, he's thinking.

She knows he likes what he's seeing but she plays it off.

"Did you like your coffee?"

"Coffee? Coffee? Oh yes, my coffee. Yes, it was delicious," he says, licking his full lips. Then the office becomes so silent you can hear snow fall.

"Sooo ... what did you want?" Gia asks, taking a seat in one of the chairs positioned in front of his desk. She places the tablet on her lap.

"Want? Oh yeah, what I want ... Oh yeah, Ms. Shirley—"

"Can you please call me Gia?"

"Ok, Gia."

"Thanks," she tells him.

"The company is having its 30th anniversary party next month. This year it's up to me to plan it."

Gia lifts the tablet up off her lap, crosses her legs making sure her skirt raises just enough for him to get a sneak peek. "Good. I love parties. What do you want me to do because I can plan the whole bash. Just give me a budget." She assures him he has the right women for the job.

"Whoo, you just took a load off my shoulders. I have so much to do around here and very little time to do it. Not to mention the fact that I have no idea how to put a small party together, more less talking about one of this magnitude."

"Well that's what you pay me for," she adds.

"The budget is $300,000. And Sherry Thompson that works across the hall ... I'm sure you two have met by now ... she has all the contact information you will need to set everything up. The party is usually held at the Mayflower hotel but you can have it at any nice venue."

"Thanks, Mr. Smith, for putting all your trust in me."

He leans back in his leather captain office chair. "You came in here wearing all these designer suits, looking like you just jumped off the cover of *Elle* magazine. Something is telling me this will be the nicest party we've ever had," he tells her, showing his perfect smile. "Are you married, Gia?"

"I was. But my husband and daughter died in a car accident two years ago," she lies.

"Wow, I'm sorry to hear that," he tells her.

"Don't be. Him and I were over. But my child I will always miss."

She is playing her role. Gia was adopted. She never met her family until she met her twin sister at a party before she got locked up. They ran into one another in the restroom. Gia was coming in and her sister was going out. They bumped into each other. Both of them jumped 'cause they're identical. They could not believe how they found one another. They talked about how they grew up and how they knew they had to have someone out there in the world that they were missing. They exchanged information and kept in contact until Gia got locked up. They lost contact until a few weeks ago when Gia ran into her at the P.O.'s office. Gia doesn't trust her, and for real she really doesn't like her too much but she respects the fact that she's her sister. Her twin did some foul shit to her in the past that she wasn't feeling

but she felt like she needed to forgive her; after all, she is her blood—the only blood she knows.

"Is there anything else I can do for you?" she asks him.

"No, that will be all."

Gia raises up, struts out his office bouncing her basket balls a little harder than normal, hoping he's looking.

I know he's watching, she's thinking as she starts to close his door behind her. Before she could get it closed:

"It may be one more thing," he says, star gazing. "Can you stay a little late tonight? I may need your help with these weekly stats."

"That wouldn't be a problem. But tonight I'm taking my father to the game to see the Wizards. How about tomorrow?" She tells another lie.

"That'a be great. Tomorrow it is. And Gia that is so nice of you to take your father to the game? How old is he?"

"Seventy. He can't walk." Another lie she tells before exiting his office.

"Damn, I hated to turn his fine ass down. He looks so freakin' good. I mean he could be my man. He reminds me of my ex. That black muthafucka could lay down the law in bed. And that Ted, his partner, looks like a George Clooney. I guess I'll have to see who has the biggest cut. Only time will tell," she whispers to herself, walking across the hall to Sherry's office.

"Hey, Sherry, I'm—"

"I know who you are. And as far as I'm concerned you're just the Temp—and it's *Ms. Thompson* to you. Here is the rolodex. And please don't ask me for help. I got enough shit to do around here. For the record, I'm not your friend. I don't wanna be. So don't ask me to eat wit' you or go out wit' you. I don't hang wit' the help," Sherry tells her in one breath.

"That's fine wit' me, secretary!" Gia snaps back.

"What did you say?"

"You heard me. Did I st-st-studda, bitch," Gia whispers, gritting on her with disgust written all over her face.

"Fuck with me, little girl, I'll have your job," Sherry whispers back through clenched teeth.

"Hell, you can have it since I know it pays more than yours," Gia strikes back as she walks out her office, back across the hall to her outer office space. "I see I'ma have'ta show and prove around here. These bitches are so jelly. But that's ok 'cause I'll be at the top of the food chain before McDonalds comes up wit' a new burger."

Day 4

"It's Wednesday, getting over the hump day. A bitch like me is sick of this 9 to 5 shit already." Gia sits in her living room talking out loud to no one but herself, as always. She picks up a paper that lays on her coffee table.

Gia has been working all day on this event. She's called venues and they are all booked; all but one—the JW Marriott. So she takes the date they have quickly. Then she calls Janet Flowers, the best in the DC area. The event planner at the hotel told her they would take care of the food. She faxed Gia over a copy of the menu. Gia picked shrimp, jumbo crab cakes, goat cheese, string beans, chicken breast, ham, champagne, a host of sweets coffee and Teas as well. She took the money to the event planner, then she called her booster Brittany to hook her up with something hot for the party. She has to go today to taste test some of the food and that she is looking forward to. She picks up her phone to call her friend. He answers.

"Hi, boo," he calls her.

"Hey, Jason. You coming through tonight?"

"I gotta pick up my daughter."

"Jason, my ass is so horny. I know you can come over for an hour or so. Can't your daughter wait?" she asks her fuck partner.

"No, Gia. And that's so selfish of you to even ask. Nobody comes before her."

"You always do this shit. I need your ass bad. Hell, it's been five days," Gia squeals.

"It hasn't. It's only been two. Besides, didn't you tell me I can't be beaten that pussy up 'cause you's a worka girl now?" he reminds her with his Jamaican accent.

"Whateva!" she shouts, then hangs up in his ear. "Men—you can't live wit'em, can't live without'em!" she screams out loud.

Rushing, she goes to her dresser drawer, she pulls out her silver bullet, lays on her bed, pulls her shorts to the side, spreads her legs apart, turns the bullet on, presses it to her hard clit to relive the feeling she's having. She moans as the vibration of the bullet caresses her kitty; it goes round and round.

"Sissss ... yes oh yes," she moans as her mind goes to ecstasy. When she's about to cum she hears the sounds of her cell ringing. She jumps up and answers it.

"Hello?"

"Gia, this is Mrs. Jones. I was just checking to see if you did all that needs to be done for the party."

Oh how I hate this bitch, Gia is thinking.

"Yes, everything is done. Mrs. Jones, it would be nice if you could wait until work hours to call me about small stuff. I do have a life, you know," Gia converses.

"Well you do work for me. I do need to know things so I'll call you when I need you," she fires back.

"Correction: I work for the company and you don't sign my check. The Temp agency does."

Click. Gia hangs up on in her ear.

"That bitch interrupting my sex session for some bullshit. But it's ok, I got a surprise that will make that old hoe pop out her eyes."

Day 5

It's Thursday morning. Gia wakes up to the birds humming and the sun shining through her large bay window.

"What time is it?" She yawns, looking over at the clock on her nightstand.

"Oh shit, I'm late! It's fuckin' eight. I'm not gon make it by 8:30, it's no way. Ok, Gia, think fast. Shit, let me call Bill ... fuck, he probably not in yet! I got it—I'll call the lady at the JW and tell her I'm going to drop in this morning."

Gia picks up her house phone, dials the event planner at the JW Marriott.

"JW Marriott, how my I direct your call?" the operator addresses.

"Yes, my name is Ms. Shirley. I'm planning a party that will take place there next month. I would like to come through this morning to check out the Ballroom."

"Ms. Shirley, let me direct your call to Mrs. Bryant. Please hold."

Gia stands by listening to the sounds of Kenny G's "Songbird."

Thirty seconds later, "Ms. Shirley, how are you today?" the chipper voice of Mrs. Bryant comes on the line.

"I'm fine, thank you."

"I hear you would like to come through this morning to check out the Ballrooms?"

"Yes, I would. If that's possible?" Gia's at her mercy.

"Ms. Shirley, that will be fine by me. Do you know what time you would like to come through?"

"About nine this morning, if that's ok with you."

"I'll clear my calendar. See you at nine this morning," Mrs. Bryant returns.

"Thanks. See you then." Gia is relived.

Now I have my excuse, Gia ponders as she gets ready.

After she's dressed, she dials her job.

"Smith, Fordham & Burt," the receptionist answers.

"This is Gia Shirley. I won't be in until 12 noon or so—"

"What's your excuse?" the receptionist quickly spits.

"None for you. But you can transfer me to Mr. Smith's voicemail, thanks," Gia politely comments.

Click.

"Oh hell no she didn't. That bitch!" Gia yells.

Then she dials the office again. After the first ring the receptionist answers.

"Smith—"

Gia cuts her off right away. "I'ma cut your tongue out your mouth and watch you die a slow death. You can count on it!" Gia whispers, then hangs up the phone laughing. "Mrs. Jones was gon' be my fist Victim but I've changed my mind. It's gon' be that ratchet ass white bitch," she murmurs while putting on her makeup, continuing to laugh.

She meets with Mrs. Bryant then she goes to work. She walks into the office straight to the receptionist desk.

"Excuse me, I think you hung up on me," Gia communicates real nice like.

"You think? Well, you not paid to think," the receptionist informs her, rolling her eyes, throwing her long blond hair back.

"I would like to call a truce. I brought you some cupcakes from Sweet Tooth's Bakery. They make the best in town," Gia says with a smile across her face.

"Well, you can put them over there. I don't want'em," she verbalizes wit' an attitude.

"Aw c'mon, they're delicious." Gia takes a bit out of one of them.

"Well maybe one of them won't hurt. I'm trying to watch my girlish figure, you know."

Gia hands her the cupcake with the red frosting on it. "Here, take this one. Red is my favorite color." Gia should have grew up in Hollywood, California, 'cause she's a great actress.

"*Ummm* ... this is good, Gia," she talks with her mouth full.

"See, I told you." Gia leaves the other cupcakes on her desk. And true to Gia's thinking, she eats one more of them. And within ten minutes …

"Uh ... uh ... *whoo* ... my stomach didn't like them cupcakes as much as my mouth did." The receptionist holds her stomach, calling over the intercom to Sherry. "Can you come and take over for me. I gotta go to the restroom, Sherry."

"Sure, I'll be right there."

When Sherry appears, the receptionist jumps up holding her stomach. She rushes to the restroom. She barely gets her skirt up and her underwear off before her turtles start to come out.

She sits on the toilet.

Bluuuu-bluuss!

She starts shitting right away. She looks up and sees Gia standing right in front of her with the stall door open.

"What you doing in here? Get out, I'm shittin'." Her stomach is cramping too much for her to even fuss.

"I just wanted to make sure you was ok," Gia tells her.

"Well I'm *ohh—Ahhhhh*."

Gia starts choking her around her neck. "You hung up on me this morning. I told you I was gon' cut your tongue out." Gia takes the tongs that's in her other hand and pinches her tongue with them. "Now hold still. I'ma make this quick and painful." Gia lets her neck go and brings her hand down with the razor blade in it, then she stops short of the tip of the receptionist's tongue. She bursts out laughing, then she lets go. The receptionist feels so relieved. She really thought Gia was going to make her tongue-less.

"That shit ain't funny, you black bitch. You scared the hell outta me! You stupid bitch!" she's yelling and pushing Gia's hands away from her. Gia glares down at her.

"I know I shouldn't have scared you like that. I'm sorry but I would never cut your tongue out. But I will do this."

Gia pulls a needle out of her pocket. Quickly she jams it in the side of her neck, pushing the poison into the receptionist's veins. She instantly keels over and dies a quick death. Gia stands over her corpse.

"I really, really wanted to keep my word and watch you die a slow death. Momma said a woman is nothing without her word. But in this case cutting your fuckin' tongue out would've been too messy. Too much blood for this time of day. You's a lucky bitch."

Gia quickly moves out the stall, washes her hands, opens the restroom door. She checks her surroundings, then makes her get away. She sashays to her desk like nothing ever happened.

Day 6

"I can't believe what happened to Lisa the receptionist," one of the ladies whispers to another co-worker in the office.

"Me either. I mean how did she die anyway?" another lady says.

"They don't know," Sherry chimes. "All I know is she called me to take over the switchboard while she went to the restroom. The damn board was so busy, time got past me. When I did look down at my watch I noticed thirty minutes had passed so I ask Danna—you know her, the red hair older lady that cleans the office?"

"Yeah," one of the ladies cuts in.

"Well, she went to see if Lisa was still in the restroom. Then all of a sudden I see Danna running towards me screaming, 'She's dead, she's dead! Her eyes still open! She's dead!' She looked like she had just saw a ghost. She grabbed her stuff and told me she quit. I got up and walked to the restroom myself. After seeing what I saw I ran to Mr. Smith's office to tell him, then that bitch Gia was like what's wrong what happened. I told her and she called the police," Sherry explains. They all gasp.

"You poor girl. You musta been shocked?" Mrs. Jones hugs her.

"Shocked is not the word, Mrs. Jones."

"Maybe she had something and she didn't tell nobody," one of the women who's eavesdropping says.

"Who knows with these young girls," Mrs. Martha, the office manager, chimes in.

"Oh well, life goes on. I have to get back to work," Sherry spits. As she turns to walk away, Gia rolls up. They exchange words.

"Who is that pretty young lady?" one of the older ladies needs to know.

"She's the new temp. She's working for Mr. Smith," Mrs. Jones returns.

"Mr. Smith is sure to fuck that one," Martha remarks.

"Martha, hush your mouth. He's a married and a very respectful man, I have you know," Mrs. Jones tells her, disgusted with what she just said in front of the other employees.

"He's not too respectful. Let's not forget he got caught with Susan in the restroom as a matter of fact. The same one they just found that girl in ... dead as a door knob."

"Remind me never to use that damn restroom again, eva in life," Janise, the head of finances, exclaims.

"But Martha you don't even know if that's true. That could've been a rumor on this job," Mrs. Jones assures them all.

"Well, he's a man with a dick that still gets hard. I don't put nothing past none of 'em. I do know that girl is bewitching and he's a sucker for a young pretty face so I think all y'all need to watch out for your jobs. Look at Susan; she was transferred to New York, and now she's our boss. So what does that tell you?"

"On that note, I'm going downstairs back to my office where life is simple," Janise mutters and bows out this time.

"That sounds good to me. As a matter of speaking, we all need to get back to work. Back to work, ladies." Martha claps her hands and orders.

***

Gia enters Bill's office.

"Mr. Smith, do you have a minute?"

"Yes, do come in. Take a seat." He's having a conversation with his partner Ted. "What is it, Gia?" Bill gives her his undivided attention.

"I just wanted to tell you I can stay late tonight if you need anything. I'm done with the project you gave me."

"Gia, you're such a good worker. I'm not going to need you tonight. Janise is going to help me in the boardroom but maybe tomorrow night," Bill informs her.

"Bill, I may need her tomorrow. I'm having trouble with the Mason account. Maybe she can do my spreadsheets for me while I go over the numbers."

"Well, Gia, would you like to help Ted?"

"Sure, why not." Her voice is real chipper. She's still standing in his office.

"Will that be all?" Bill is short with her.

"Yes, Sir," she tells him, walking out of his off.

I'm going to fuck his brains out. And Bill you're going to be next. They just don't know who they hired.

Day 7

It's a new day. The sun is shining, the weather crisp. Gia is feeling well rested as she makes a beeline to her office. She places her fresh flowers in the empty vase that sets on her desk, then she does her everyday duties—pours Mr. Smith a hot black cup of decaf coffee, sets it on his desk ever so gently, turns his computer on, pulling the day's rates up.

She goes back to her office, turns on her computer, pulling up the work for today. Gia's really loving her job but she wants the top position. She does her job well as she tiptoes around all the haters, but this is something she's been accustomed to all her life. This is nothing she can't handle. Plus she's not a people person anyway.

She makes her last phone call, then puts in her last report.

"Gia, you're doing a good job. I wish you were here a long time ago. My workload is so much lighter now that we've found you," Bill compliments her.

"Thank you, Sir—"

"Gia, please call me Bill. You're my assistant, the closest person to me right now so do call me Bill," he retorts.

"Whatever you say, Bill." She smiles.

"I'm leaving for tonight but remember you told Ted you would help him with those spreadsheets. If it's anything you don't understand you let him know. I'm sure Harvard University prepared you for anything he shoots your way."

I almost forgot I put Harvard on my app.

"Yes they did. I can' wait to see what he has in store for me tonight."

Even though she lied to the Temp company about where she got her credentials, when she was in the military they put her through school. She earned her Accounting degree then she went to Howard University and earned her Masters. Gia knows more than most of the workers in the department.

Leaning over he whispers in her ear, "You'll do great. But Gia don't show him out. Let him feel like he knows a little something," Gia hears him but then again she doesn't 'cause she's too busy enjoying the smell of his cologne.

"I won't, I promise."

Everyone has left, even the cleaning crew. Gia goes to the restroom, giving herself a makeover. She returns to her desk, flicks her light switch to off, then paces herself towards Ted's office.

Knock, knock. She knocks on his door that's ajar.

"Hi, Gia, come in," he says, sitting behind his desk scanning his computer.

The lovely Gia struts her way across his office dressed in a Pink Prabal Gurung dress priced at $3,200. She's also sporting some Jil Sander shoes, priced at $900. Gia looks the part even though she didn't pay full price but who knows that but her and her booster. She takes a seat in the chair adjacent from his desk.

"What is it you would like for me to do?" she asks, licking the top of her lips just so, making sure she doesn't mess up her natural color Lip Gloss by Nass.

"If you come over here I can show you these damn spreadsheets. They're a piece of work."

"Sure." She gets up, making her way over to join Ted. She bends over him so she can get a close look at what it is he wants her to do. He starts explaining what he needs done.

"These are the spreadsheets. You have to make sure the number on this side of the spreadsheet matches this side. You also have to be careful 'cause some of the numbers look alike but they're not."

"If they don't match, then what?" she asks.

"Then you'll have to go to that computer over there." He points at a table that's in front of his window. "That computer is the Error in the Hole computer. You input the bad number and it gives you a new number to add to this sheet. After you put the new number on this sheet it will be added to what we call the Blackout list."

"Oh, is that the Department downstairs?" she quizzes.

He looks up at her. Their eyes bounce off one another's.

"Gia, I'm married." He feels he has to tell her. She acts like she doesn't hear a word he's saying by cutting him off. She places her lips over his, making sure she covers his whole mouth.

"Oh my God," Ted mumbles, feeling his nature raising.

Gia caresses his hard penis with the tips of her fingers.

"Yes, that's what I'm talking 'bout. Nice and hard. Now where were we?" She's running her fingers through his jet black silky hair.

Ted just sits there speechless. Gia moves the papers that's in front of him to the side of his desk, then hops up on it, leaning back on her elbows. She opens her legs so Ted can see the pinkness of her pussy. Ted becomes broken as he sees her freshly manicured pussy hairs. She has them cut into one straight line. She places her right hand on her right tender young breast then she licks and sucks the hard nipple that's before her. Ted stands and pulls his pants all the way off, exposing his tighty whities. He's positioned in front of her, massaging his little six-inch pink dick through his undies. Gia scoots to the edge of the desk, eager to get this over with.

"Put it in my wet pussy, big daddy." She feeds his ego. Ted pulls his whites off and does just that. He slides his little man inside her wetness, taking in the warmth of her body. He exhales. He starts to move slowly, rolling his eyes to the back of his head, rocking back and forth on his heels.

"Ohh this feels so good," he repeats over and over until his mouth feels like cotton.

I wish this muthafucka would hurry up and cum already wit' this little ass dick, are her thoughts.

Gia relaxes her head backward, closes her eyes thinking if she just relaxes and thinks of a big black dick maybe she can get some enjoyment out of it.

"Fuck me ... fuck me, daddy!" she moans.

Ted starts to pick up the pace a bit.

"Yes, baby. Make love to this pussy. Give it to me, baby ... shit, fuck this pussy," she acts out as Ted thrusts in and out.

"Oh, Gia, Gia, Gia," Ted whispers.

Ted starts pumping faster, rocking the desk. Papers are falling on the floor. Ted grabs Gia around her neck, squeezing tightly. Now Gia is waking up as her body starts to tingle.

"*Uhmmmm ... mmmm* shit! Ted, get this pussy. That's what a bitch talking 'bout," she mummers through breaths. He grabs her neck harder as he feels himself getting ready to release his fluids inside her.

"Gia, I'm cumming, Teddy's cumming!" he yells. "Shit oh shit!" Ted continues to yell as he shoots his nut all in her hot pussy.

But Gia continues to grind on his soft dick, causing it to get back up. She thrusts and grinds on his dick for about five minutes.

"Gia, Gia, oh my Gia, I'm cumming again!" Ted groans, filling the walls of her wetness with his cum, one more time.

"Me too ... daddy more-bucks, me too." She's lying. "Oh, Ted, taste my cum," she demands. Ted pulls his dick out, kneels, sucking all Gia's cum out her pussy. Then he stands up and jerks his dick as he raises to his tiptoes. Gia jumps off his desk, bends over and sucks his dick.

"Awwwwh shit, Gia. Oh my goodness here I cum." Ted squirts nut in Gia's mouth. She gargles then she stands and places her mouth over his, allowing his nut to flow from her mouth to his. She hawk eyes him.

"Now *you* swallow," she tells him with a devilish smirk on her face.

Ted is good at following orders.

Day 8

Two down. Ted is so high off my pussy he doesn't know what to do. We fucked until ten last night, then he called my cell at 12 midnight, as if he could come over. His ass is gone already. "Damn, kitty, you really got his ass purring, didn't you?" she says, looking down at her pussy, nodding her head like what a shame

Ring.

Who in the hell is it at this time of the morning?

"Hello?" she answers.

"Hi, may I speak with Ms. Shirley?"

"This is she."

"Hi, Ms. Shirley, this is Mrs. Bryant from the JW."

"Hi, how may I help you this early in the morning?" Gia is being funny.

"I was calling to ask you if you would like two types of toss greens, because you ordered the one that has nuts in the ingredients," she informs her.

"I know, I picked the menu." Gia's baffled.

"Well when I checked the roster I found that you all have an employee that is allergic to nuts."

"Oh really, who might that person be?"

"Let me see here ... here it is ... A Mrs. Jones, Mrs. Allen Jones," the events planner tells her.

"That's too bad. We'll have to change that then. Go ahead and add the one without nuts as well. Thank you for the information 'cause that could've been fatal." Gia acts concern.

"It's nothing. That's my job, but you're welcome."

"Is there anything else I need to know, Mrs. Bryant?"

"No, I think that covers it, but if I run across anything else I'll call you for sure," she tells Gia all chipper like. Then they end their call.

"She's allergic to nuts, huh?" Gia says to herself as she goes back to eating her breakfast.

After eating, she takes a shower then gets dressed. She hops in her car, headed to Dan's Bakery. Pulling up 15 minutes later she parks her car, walks inside.

"Hey, Dan, long time no see," she greets. He's standing behind his backer counter with a white apron on and a long white chef hat on his head.

"Why hello, Vicky. It's been too long." Vicky is the name Gia gave him when she fucked his brains out two months ago. "Damn, you looking rich and fine as ever."

"Thanks."

"What brings you through?"

"Dan, I need a cake baked with peanuts in it crushed up real fine. I don't want to be able to see them. My client is funny about crunching on nuts. I don't want her to be able to taste them either. I'm trying to turn her on to some new things but I want it to be pleasing to her at the same time. You know what I mean?"

"Boy, do I," Dan says with lust in his eyes. "When would you like this cake?"

"Lunch time. Can you make that happen?" she asks, pulling up her skirt exposing her Mohawk pussy.

"Yeah, anything for an old friend." He smiles.

***

Thirty minutes has passed. Gia walks out the bakery feeling refreshed.

That Dan sho can eat some kat. I came three times. Damn, if he wasn't so broke I would marry his ass then kill'em for the insurance policy but his policy is only worth $100,000. That's why I stopped fucking his ass in the first place, but this kill will be worth all the head he just gave me and more, she's thinking as she starts up her car.

She calls the office to let her boss know she's going to be in at one because she has to stop past the JW to handle some of the arrangements. He tells her he'll see her when she gets in to take her time.

Gia does some window shopping, grabs some lunch then heads back to Dan's bakery, picking up the cake. She heads for work—of course after Dan licks her kitty one more time.

She reaches her office, sways in, greets the new receptionist then she stops by Mrs. Allen Jones' office. Gia sticks her head in the door.

"Good, no one's here." She places the cake on the desk, grabs a sticky paper, writes a note. *Thanks for all your hard work, you know who.* She also draws a happy face on it. She lays it on the cake box then she makes her exit unnoticed.

Day 9

"Martha, come here, come here," Janise calls her in a low voice from her office.

"What, girl why we whispering?" Martha whispers.

"Shut the door," she tells her friend. Martha does just that.

"Did you hear?"

"Here what?"

"It's Allen. She's in a coma."

"A what!" Martha's dumbfounded.

"One of the girls from the mailroom found her unconscious on her office floor yesterday. The police been in here all morning. You just missed them."

"On the floor unconscious?! What happened, how did she fall out?" Martha huffs.

"I don't know but I'ma get to the bottom of it."

"What do you mean to the bottom of it? You think somebody did something to'a?" Martha adds all big-eyed.

"No, they say she's allergic to peanuts and that's what the doctors found in her system."

"Peanuts? Why on earth would she eat'em if she's allergic to'em?" Martha's lost.

"They say it was an unfinished cake on her desk with crumbs around her mouth. Rick from the Blackout accounts said she offered him some. He told the police he didn't taste no peanuts in the cake. He added that the damn cake was good. When they asked him did he know where she got the cake from he told them he didn't know. Then they questioned Bill and Ted. They said they didn't know how she got the cake. Then they asked all of us if we gave it to her 'cause it was a note on her desk somebody wrote her, as if someone from here gave her the cake as a reward for her good work. They are asking that we all do a handwriting analysis. That bitch Sherry told them you may have given her the cake since you two are close. Girl, it's getting' hot in *herre*!"

"Me ...? I didn't get her no cake. Why didn't anyone call me last night or this morning to tell me about this shit?!"

"I'on know but this I do know: shit getting' ready to hit the fan," Janise murmurs.

"Do you think somebody's tryna kill'a?" Martha is still stuck on stupid.

"Like I said ... I don't know, but this I do know: first it was that poor receptionist, now it's Allen. If you put two and two together all this shit didn't start until that Temp girl came." Janise is being messy.

"My God! You think she's a killer? But why ... why would she kill a receptionist? It's nothing to gain by killing her. She's already making more, and the girl wears expensive clothes. Hell I can't even afford the stuff she wears." Martha lets it be known.

"I hear she's dating one of them gangsta guys ... you know, a drug dealer." Janise is making stuff up now.

Martha gasps, covering her mouth with her hand. But little do they both know Gia is standing outside the door.

"Knock ... knock," Gia voices as she opens Janise's door. She enters, smiling.

"Hi, how are you?" Martha inquires, clearing her throat.

"I hope I didn't interrupt anything important," Gia says.

"Oh no. How can we help you, Ms. Gia?" Janise parts her lips, glancing over at Martha to let her know that is Gia, even though she knows already.

"In light of everything that's happened around here, I bought this card and some flowers for Allen's family. Would you two like to sign it?" Gia remarks, holding out the card and a black pen towards them.

"Why yes, I think that's nice of you, Gia, being as though you just got here," Janise huffs, not buying the nice girl act one bit.

They both sign the card.

"Thanks." Gia begins to withdraw herself from the office, then she looks back. "Oh yeah, Mrs. Martha, I was wondering if you could help me with some work Mr. Smith gave me. Some of the numbers I'm not too sure of. Since you've been here for 20 years. Well, I—"

"Say no more, honey. Of course Martha will help you. Won't you, Martha," Janise interrupts Gia while glancing over at her longtime friend reading her facial expression.

"What time?" Gia probes Martha.

"How about tonight around six. You can meet me at Gladys Knight's Chicken & Waffles. Do you know where it is?" Martha quizzes.

"No, but I have a friend that eats there all the time. I'll find it."

"That's good. Don't forget to bring your files." Janise is being messy again.

"I won't. Thank you so much," Gia tells the two of them as she scampers from the office. "They think they're going to stop shit. I got some'em for they asses," Gia mumbles under her breath as she makes her way back to her desk. She hits her intercom button.

"Bill, I have to make a run. May I have the rest of the day off?"

"Sure, but can you send flowers to my wife first. It's our anniversary, I almost forgot."

"Congratulations," she tells him.

"Thanks."

"I'll have to give you a gift."

"That will be all, Gia," he rudely says.

"Did I offend you?"

"No, you could never do that."

"Ok, have a good night," she chirps.

"I will, thanks."

He's playing hard to get but he'll break. They all do, she thinks while placing the call to the florist.

Day 10

It's 7:00 a.m. Gia's sitting in her living room watching TV.

I'm so happy we're off this weekend. That damn job works you like'a slave, she thinks, placing her cup of tea between her pouched lips.

"Good morning and welcome to ABC News Center. We bring you troubling news this morning as Rhonda Chung reports from Suitland, Maryland. Hi Ronda."

"Hi Mack, I'm reporting live in front of Don's Bakery, where Maryland police are investigating Don the baker's death. He was found this morning with a gunshot wound to the head. No one seemed to hear anything. It's a sad day in this quiet part of town. Don's Bakery was a trademark here in Suitland Shopping Center. Other business owners are shocked, saying Don was a good man and he did many things for the neighborhood children. This community is very upset about this sad and costly tragedy. Police are asking if anyone has seen or heard anything. Please contact the local authorities. Mack, back to you."

"I can't believe this. They found him already," Gia sits back in her chair whispering to herself. "My pussy sho gon' miss his tongue but he had to go 'cause I know his ass would've talked. When Bill told me the police was going to Dan's bakery to find out who bought that type of cake I know I had to kill'em. Why did he have to order platters with his company name and logo? They would've never knew where the cake came from. He would be still alive to this day. Now I gotta get Mrs. Martha's ass. She canceled our dinner date until tomorrow but she's as good as gone. She just don't know it yet."

Tap tap tap. Someone is at Gia's front door.

"Who's there?"

"It's me."

"Here I come!" Gia yells as she rises and opens her door. "Hi, baby, do come in," she yaps in a sexy way.

"Hi, yourself," Ted welcomes, hugging Gia around her tiny waist.

"Um ... you want some morning pussy, don't you?"

"You know daddy do." He cheeses with pleasure.

"I was thinking we do something new," she lets out.

"And what might that be?"

"Are you down for what eva?" She has a smirk on her face.

"You know it."

Only if he knew what he just signed up for.

They go to her room.

"Ok, take off all your clothes. Put on this blindfold," she demands.

"Oh, you're getting kinky on me." Ted does what's asked of him.

She pulls out white handcuffs. "Lay on the bed, face down," she directs.

She handcuffs both wrists and ankles to the bedpost.

"Gia, what are you going to do with me?" He's getting curious.

"Don't worry, daddy. We're gon' have ourselves a ball." She giggles. "Now you wait right there."

Gia returns in about one minute flat. Ted is lying on the bed, ass up.

"I'm back, baby. Now tell me how this feels."

In seconds Ted feels a wet long tongue licking his asshole over and over really fast. Ted's ass wiggles.

"Aw ... uh oh ... yes, Gia, right there that feels so good," Ted moans.

"Lift your butt in the air," she directs.

He does it. With her hand full of warm gel she reaches around him and starts jerking his small dick.

"Yes, baby, yes. Gia baby, you're going to make Big Teddy milky."

He must mean little teddy, she thinks as she continues to please him. He's not prepared for what comes next.

"Awwww, Aweee *noooo*!" Ted yells as his ass starts to raise up and down from the unwanted actions she's delivering.

"Oh, Ted, stop grumblin'. Relax. Relax. This is the best part."

"Awww! Gia, that shit hurts. What is it?"

"I know it hurts. Baby but you said you wanted to play. It'll feel better soon," Gia promises as she continues to ram the nine-inch rubber dildo in and out his ass.

After a while Ted starts catching the rhythm of the handheld dildo. Ted starts to relax as the hole of his ass opens wider with every stroke. His dick starts to jump as it grows hard as a rock.

"Oh shit, Gia, shit!" is all he can say as nut flows from his penis onto her white sheet. Tears flow down his checks from the shame of enjoying the unnatural sexual escapade that's unfolding right before him.

"You like that, baby?" Gia asks. As much as he hated to admit it, he does. "You want more?"

"I do. I do. Please, I do." Ted becomes shameless.

"Not now. We're going to do something different."

"What eva you say."

Gia pulls the dick out Ted's ass. "I'll be right back, daddy. Now don't you move," she says in a childlike voice.

Then she grabs a glass case off the table. She returns to his bedside.

"I'm back. Now where were we?" she utters.

Gia spreads Ted's ass cheeks apart, lubing his asshole really good with warm gel.

"Yes, Gia. Now that feels really good. It's nothing like a butt massage. Gia, please your daddy," he mummers.

"I am. I am." She pulls out a baby gerbil, puts it at the tip of Ted's asshole.

"You ready?" She giggles.

Yes, yes, he eagerly nods.

"Here we go." She lets the gerbil go. It enters his ass head first.

"OOOOOOOh! Noooooo! No what's that I don't like it Gia what is it?!"

Ignoring his cries, she picks up the next one and lets it loose. Ted is howling and squealing.

"AHHHH! STOP MY GOD WHAT IS IT?!" Ted is squirming but he can't get loose.

"Relax, Ted, and enjoy it. My boyfriends love this game. It's called the mousetrap. Let's see how many you can hold."

"GIA, PLEASE! I don't like this one! Go get the dildo please I will let you fuck me again with it, but not this! What is that?! I can feel it moving in my stomach, Gia! I don't want it in me, PLEASE! I don't like this!" he yells.

Warm streams of salt water flow down his face.

"Ted, they're just little baby gerbils. I can go get their mother and father," she teases.

"Ger—WHAT DID YOU SAY A GERBIL?! Gia ... Gia please don't ... do this to me, STOP! It's not fun anymore!"

"Ok you little baby boy." Gia places cheese at the tip of his ass, summoning the gerbils. She places them back in the glass case as they come out one by one. She removes his blindfold.

"Now before I uncuff you, you have to lick me dry." Gia loves herself some good head.

"Ok … ok," he says, embarrassed and relieved all at the same time.

After he pleasures her, she gets up.

"We done, right? I can go?" he asks, hoping the answer would be yes.

"Yeah, you party pooper. After I go to the bathroom I'll uncuff your baby ass." She's irritated so she pouts all the way to the next room, pulling out the recorded tape.

"I got you now ... you son of a bitch. I'll be head of control by next week. Men—they're so dumb," Gia chats to herself, putting the tape in her hiding spot.

Day 11

Gia stops by the coffee shop to pick up some donuts. She strolls up to the counter.

"Good morning. I need two dozen donuts, please."

"What kind would you like?" the cashier asks.

"The same as I always get."

"I'm new. I just started toda—"

"I'll take care of her," one of the other workers says. She starts fixing Gia's usual.

"Gail Rice!" one of the customers yells out, making her way to face Gia. "Gail!" she howls again, tapping Gia on her shoulder.

Gia swings around, searching the lady over like she's crazy. "Excuse me?" Gia utters.

"You don't remember me? It's Pattie from Wilson and Johnson. You know Pattie girl your old manager. I'm sorry about how Peter did you. He shouldn't have fired you like that. It's just that so much was going on and all the accusations against you and him. His wife—"

"You must be mistaken. I'm not Gail nor do I know any one named Gail. Most of all I don't know a Pattie or a Peter." Gia acts baffled.

"I'm sorry. You look just like her, beautiful as ever. But you're right because Gail got locked up for hacking Wilson and Johnson's computers. She tapped into the government computers as well, through one of our biggest client's accounts. That's when Peter started letting people go. The company became bankrupt," she yaps in one breath.

"I'm sorry to hear that. Maybe one day you will find the lady you seem eager to tell all this unwanted information," Gia delivers with a slight smile across her face.

"That will be $12.50," the cashier chimes in after rubbernecking.

Gia hurries and pays her bill then flees the shop.

"What in the hell is Pattie doing in DC? Shit, that was when I was in Texas. This world is too gotdamn small. You can't even relocate to rid yourself of cockroaches. I'm thinking should I double back and exterminate her ass?" Gia utters to herself, opening her car door.

***

Forty minutes later Gia is pulling into the garage of her job. She parks her car on the lower deck, pulls a silver vibrating bullet out her purse. She glances out her car window, taking stock of her surroundings.

"Boy do I need you. I'm so mad and horny I need to relieve all this tension." She's talking to herself again.

Lifting her skirt up, pulling her thong to the side, she places the bullet on her clit just so and flips the switch. After about 1 minute in heaven,

"Noooo ... oh HELL NO! My fuckin' batteries ran out. *Shit.* I need some fuckin' batteries." She's going crazy looking through her glove compartment, on the floor, in the ash tray, she's digging in her purse.

All of a sudden—*tap, tap.*

She jumps with the bullet in hand. She starts her car up to let down the window.

"What is it, Sherry?" she snaps with irritation.

Sherry grins, holding up a pack of batteries. "You need these. Ha ha ha," she starts laughing her ass off.

"Fuck you, bitch," Gia shouts, letting her window back up.

I'm gon kill'a. If it's the last thing I do, she tells herself.

Gia lets herself out of her car, grabbing hold of the donuts. She heads into the office. Everyone is looking at her funny but Gia is being Gia, letting on like she notices nothing at all.

She peeps in his office. "Good morning, Bill," she greets.

"Good morning, Gia. Can you make sure everyone is in the boardroom by 10:00 this morning?"

"Will do, Sir," she said to Bill.

"Thanks. Put the receipt on Sherry's desk for the donuts so we can reimburse you," he tells her, never looking up.

"No problem." She carries out his orders.

It's 10:00 a.m. Everyone is gathered in the huge boardroom that's stationed on the 4th floor of the building. Ted makes his way in, then Bill, who takes a seat in between Martha and Janise at the table.

"Ok, everyone. First of all I'm proud to say that all the department heads have been really doing a great job in spite of what has transpired over the last couple of weeks. I must inform you all that Allen Jones is doing better. She is still in and out of her coma but the doctors thinks she will come around."

They all clap, including Gia.

"However, a company of this magnitude must go on in spite of. Now I don't mean to sound insensitive but we must hire a new person for control. Mrs. Jones is a very good employee and manager. We shall never forget that. But we must fill her position. If she should return, well ... we'll cross that bridge when it comes. My partners Bill Smith, Charlie Burt and myself really feel like Martha Seamen would be the perfect person for the position."

Gia's face goes from smiles to shit. *I'll fuck you up. You promised me a better position.*

Ted continues, “Now the person that will fill Martha’s position, we choose Janise Thompson.”

They all fake clap again.

“Mrs. Thompson’s position will be held by Sherry Wong. Mrs. Wong’s position goes to Gia Shirley.”

“What?! What?!” Gia yells over the loud clapping. All eyes fall on her. “I mean what, I can’t believe it. I just started here and I’m an administrative assistant already. Wow, you all really looked out. Making me part of this family. Thanks so much, Sirs.” She fakes a smile, taking a seat. Her blood is boiling.

“It was Janise’s idea.” He hits her with a low blow, thinking about the little gerbil trick.

“There’s some cake, punch and donuts. Eat up.”

The bosses exit the room. People start whispering and gossiping. Gia exits as well. She’s so pissed she doesn’t know what hit her. She wants Allen’s position so Martha will have to go is all she can think about while entering the restroom. She starts pacing the floor, biting on her bottom lip, hitting the walls. Gia has lost her mind.

Day 12

"How do you like your new desk and office?" Sherry inquires as Gia sets up her new very small office.

"It'll do for now," Gia yawps.

"I don't know about you but I love my new office, this little office ... well, if you call it an office. It was cramping my style. I knew I would move up soon." Gia sizes her up as she continues to talk. "Gia, you can always look at it this way—even though you don't get overtime now and you have this small ass office, at least you do have a job with benefits. I know the Temp agency paid more overtime but $40,000 a year isn't bad for starters," she tells Gia like she cares.

"You know what, Sherry? You're so right. Thank you. I never looked at it that way, Sherry," Gia calls her name as she arranges her flowers, setting them in her small window seal. She pauses and turns, giving Sherry a stare. "I can call you Sherry, right?" Now Gia waits for her permission with her brow raised.

"Sure."

"Can we be friends? You know, start fresh? I'm part of the family now?"

Sherry can't believe her ears. "We sure can. I thought you'd never ask."

"Good. That makes me feel much better. Why don't you stop passed my office tonight around six. We can have some drinks. You know, to celebrate our new accomplishments," Gia invites, holding up a bottle of champagne and two flute glasses.

"Hell yeah, girl. Now you talking. Hell, we can pop the cork now," she tells Gia.

"Girl, I wish. Mr. Smith would have our heads if we drink during business hours," Gia reminds her who they work for.

"I guess you're right. So meet me in my office at six. Much more space," Sherry jokes, observing her old office. "You know we'll have to be quick 'cause I've gotta meet my mother by seven."

"Oh, it will be very quick," Gia lets her know, moving her head up and down as if she knows something Sherry doesn't.

"Alright, see you then!" Sherry exclaims with cheer.

"Yes, I'll see you then," Gia returns.

Day 13

It's six on the nose. Everyone in the office has left for today. Gia grabs the bottle of champagne, heads down the hall to Sherry's office, strutting up to Sherry's desk.

"Hey, girl, I'm almost done. Have a seat," Sherry acknowledges.

Gia takes a seat at the round table that sits in the middle of Sherry's office. No more than two minutes pass. Sherry joins her.

"Thanks for wanting to be my friend. I never had one. You know, since my father died. He was the only friend I had," Sherry tells her.

"He was?"

"Yeah, my boyfriend left me. We were together since 6th grade but he left me for a white lady fifteen years older than him."

"Damn, now that's fucked up," Gia lets on like she really cares.

"Yeah, but the crazy thing is I still love him and I have to see him every day."

"Why every day?" Gia wonders.

"He works here. You may have seen him. Ricky. He's head of the Blackout accounts. He's married to Janise."

"Janise? Old lady Janise? So that's why she don't like being called Mrs. She's tryna stay young. Old hag. But she is nice. So maybe I should be nice." Gia tries to throw her off.

"That bitch ain't nice. She slept with Ted to move her way to the top and she took my man. Now she's sleeping with Ted again. I don't know what she has over'em but whatever it is she's using it. How do you think she got her job? She only has a high school diploma, and for that position you need a master's degree." She gives Gia the 411.

"That's some heavy shit you just laid on me."

"Yeah it is, being as though I have my masters and I've applied for that job three times over."

"It looks like you need to drop down and get yo eagle, girl," Gia teases and starts laughing.

"Never that. Only lowlife hoes do shit like that, feel me?" Janise says, sipping on her bubbly.

"I feel you. But I've gotta get this stuff outta my old desk and meet with Bill—I mean Mr. Smith," Gia corrects herself.

"Bill? Bill left ... he's gone to New York," she informs Gia.

"New York? Why didn't he tell me that?"

"Did you miss the memo? You don't work for him anymore. If you check your email you'll find his memo about going to the New York office. Most of the time he'll leave all the staff a memo on the internet. He left about thirty minutes ago. He's going to that office to see his wife and his old flame." Sherry is trying to let her know about Bill's past.

"I know about his old flame, which was his old assistant. But his wife works in the New York office?"

"Yep. Charlie Burt, that's his ex-wife but we still call her the wife 'cause they act like they're still married," she informs. "She never changed her name to Smith."

"But I just sent flowers to his wife at his home here in DC." Gia is baffled.

"That's his real wife. Get this: she stays home and takes care of his ex mother-in-law while his ex-wife is in New York for six months at a time. Every year for their anniversary Charlie sends the ex-wife flowers, diamonds and furs. It's a strange relationship, I must admit myself. They have some secret past. I don't know what it is but he loves her and she loves him. They will do anything for one another. But whatever happened 20 something years ago he never forgave her. He married Betty. We think 'cause she has money. *Old* money. Charlie's late father is the founder of this company. Now Bill has more shares in this company than her father. For some reason he left the company to Bill and Bill brought Ted on, then later Charlie came into play. Now get this: Charlie's ass is bisexual so who knows what's going on wit' them all." Janise spills all the gossip.

"Girl, now that's a *Lifetime* story within itself," Gia yaps.

"It sho nuff is."

They giggle.

"See you. And thanks for the 411," Gia utters, making her way out the door after downing the rest of her drink.

Sherry isn't that bad at all. Maybe she'll get to keep her life. As far as Mrs. Burt … so she's a woman—and she's gay. I must pay her a visit. Nothing like doing the boss's wife. That shit sounds like fun, Gia thinks to herself as she enters her tiny office.

Day 14

Gia walks in PG hospital.

"Those are beautiful flowers you have," the nurse on the third floor compliments.

"Oh, thank you. They're for a wonderful and dear person to me."

"And who might that be?" the nurse asks Gia.

"Mrs. Jones. Allen Jones."

"Oh, yes. Mrs. Jones. She's in room 340. You know she came out of her coma two days ago."

Gia plays it off because that's news to her ears. "Yes, I know. That's why I'm here to see her."

"Now you must know her breathing is still a little short. We've been taking her on and off the breathing machine so please don't have her talking a lot 'cause she loves to talk," the nurse adds.

"I will keep that in mind … Mrs. Day," Gia says after reading her badge.

"Oh, where you from?" the nurse asks.

"Mississippi."

"That's the country twang."

"Yes, it comes out now and again." Gia acts it out to the tee.

"We supposed to take your name and ID but I'll let you go. Your hands are full and you seem like a nice young lady."

"That's mighty kind of you, Mrs. Day. I'll just be a few. I know she needs to get much rest."

Gia walks to Allen's room. When she enters, Allen looks up at Gia and tries to say hi. Gia rushes her, pulling her pillow from under her head. Allen is bewildered. She has no idea what is going on. Her eyes widen, she's breathing rapidly. With a firm grip, Gia places the pillow over her mouth. Allen is moving around like a fish out of water as Gia smothers her to death. When she sees Allen stop moving she lifts the pillow, bends over, putting her ear to her mouth to see if she is still breathing.

"Good, that's that. Sorry, I can't have any witness," she whispers, placing the pillow back under her head neatly.

She fixes her clothes, walks out the room, taking the stairway so no one will see her. Gia hurries to her car, gets in, drives off expeditiously.

She pulls into a gas station about 20 minutes down the road, goes in the restroom, pulls out a plastic bag, takes off her wig, glasses, blue contacts, bamboo earrings and she

changes her clothes. She places everything in the bag, then she exits the restroom, hops back in her car, drives down the road. She turns into an alley and dumps the evidence in a big construction Dumpster. Then it's off to work. Gia walks in the office looking and smelling good as if nothing happened a few hours ago.

"Hi, Gia, I put a stack of folders on your desk. Mrs. Janise Thompson wants to see you," Mr. Smith's new Administrative Assistant informs her.

"Thanks." She goes to Janise's office. "You wanted to see me?" Gia stands at her desk.

"Yes. The files that are on your desk, please input the info then print it and put it on all the department heads' desks by Monday. So that means the weekend is work for you."

Gia takes her orders but she's not liking it. She hates to work on her off days.

She walks back to her office. Before she enters, she heads back to Bill's office area.

"Cathy, you know what? When I make it to the top I'm taking you with me," she informs his new assistant.

"I would love to work for you, Gia," she says with a smile. "Oh, I almost forgot Mr. Ricky Thompson would like for you to come to his office to pick up the Blackout list."

"Thanks. Can you call him to let him know I'm on my way? Can you inform Sherry in about 30 minutes? Tell her that he would also like to see her. I forgot to tell her last night. I was supposed to have met her in her office at six, but I got busy."

"Will do," Cathy returns.

Gia rides the elevator to the second floor. The elevator doors open.

Fuck, his floor is huge. And who in the hell are all these people? Where they come from? I've neva seen any of 'em before, she thinks to herself as she walks up to the receptionist desk.

"Hi, how may I help you?"

"I'm Gia Shirley from—"

"I know who you are. It's a pleasure to meet you. Mr. Thompson is waiting for you in his office. It's down that hall, make a left then a right, then another left. You can't miss it. It's the huge oval office," she directs.

"Ma'am what goes on, on this floor?" Gia needs to know.

"This is where all the out of state claims are worked on. Twelve states to be exact," the lady informs her.

"Is that right? Who is in charge of these accounts?"

"Charlie Burt. This is their department. She comes to town every six months. She's a doll."

"Yes, I heard. Well thanks for the info. I guess I'll make my way to his office."

"Anytime, Mrs. Shirley."

***

Gia strolls in Ricky's office. "You called? You wanted to see me?"

Ricky's not a bad looking brother, with his dark skin six five, wavy hair, full goatee, low cut sideburns and a full beard neatly groomed. He turns around, sitting in his office chair.

"Don't I always?" he answers with a sexy voice.

Gia smiles as she moves up to her old sex partner, leaning across the front of his desk. He knew her five years earlier. They met in New Jersey.

"So I finally met wifey and the ex. That would be baby momma. She was filling me in on some of your little secrets. I see you haven't changed one bit," Gia tells him.

"Now, now, little Gia. Let's not waste time talking," he tells her, pulling out his manhood.

"*Mmm,* my little friend. Shit, he still looks good enough to eat." She licks her lips.

"Huh, your friend misses those lips too," he returns.

Gia slowly walks around the desk. She turns Ricky's oversized office chair around, gets on her knees, taking hold of his soft dick, placing it in between her lips. His dicks grows in seconds from the wetness, the sizzling heat of her tongue. She's enjoying all nine inches of his pretty dick. As she gives him long slow strokes, she looks into his eyes.

"You like?" she says with half her mouth full.

"Indeed. Indeed I do," he informs, moving his head up and down.

Gia gets off her knees, turns, unties her brown wrap dress, allowing it to fall to the floor exposing her two perfect round shaped ass cheeks.

"Yes, *oh yes,*" he moans, resting his head on the chair, straightening his legs out.

Gia straddles him backwards. She lowers her pussyhole to the head of his huge black dick. She lowers and lowers, then she butterflies his dick back and forth to the tip and back down over and over, real slow. He meets her every stroke as he pumps, slowing to her rhythm.

"*Ummm* yes, Rick. Yes, baby *pleazz* don't stop," she begs as she continues to wind on his dick.

"Turn around, Gia," he demands of her in a low soft voice. Ricks lifts her up in the air with his masculine arms, sticking his dick back in her dripping hot wet ripe pussy. He strokes and strokes every morsel of her tenderness.

"Oh shit fuck me that's it right there don't stop *please.* Oh Rick, damn I needed this!" she's yelling now, not giving a damn who hears her.

He stuffs her underwear in her mouth to shut her up. Rick's banging and pushing, pumping and thrusting his king-size dick up in her.

"Gia. Hell, Gia, you the only bitch that can take this dick on. Oh shit, Gia." He slides his dick out and slides it in her asshole. The feeling he's delivering is astonishing. She can't hold back anymore.

"Rick, here it comes! Here it comes!"

"Nut, baby, nut!" he tells her. He looks up towards the door. "What the fuck?!" he utters, but he doesn't stop. His eyes are fixated on the person that's staring at him but he can't stop, he's gotta get his nut first. Gia is in another world. She continues to enjoy the dick he's putting on her.

"Rick, *my ass my ass,* I'm cumming!" she yells out.

"*Awww* shit, Gia, baby. Me too, me too!" he whispers, pulling his dick out after about 3 more strokes. He lowers Gia onto the floor.

Sherry is stuck. She doesn't know what to say. As Gia puts her thug on and fixes her dress, she notices Rick is staring at the door while he's pulling his pants up. He's not saying a word. She follows his eyes.

"Sherry, nice of you to join us. How long you been standing there?" Gia knows full well she told Cathy to tell her to meet Rick in 30 minutes.

When she musters up some spit, "You BITCH!" Sherry says through clinched teeth while standing in the doorway of Rick's office holding onto the knob.

"You ain't neva lied about that," Gia says. She's laughing.

Sherry looks at Rick and shakes her head. "The more things change the more they stay the same. Rick, what if it was your wife that walked in the door on you? Oh, I almost forgot—would you care? Hell, Ted's boning her anyway," Sherry spits venom then she exits his office, slamming the door.

Rick looks at Gia. "She never comes down here during the day. Never."

Gia gives him a shy look, hunching her shoulders.

"Oh no you didn't," he tells her.

"Oh but I did."

"Gia, not cool. Not cool at all."

"It's nothing I can't handle. You know how I do it."

"No, Gia, this ain't New Jersey and I don't know how you do it."

"Forget about her. I have something I need you to help me with."

"What might that be?" he asks, irritated now.

"I want you to help me make it to the top."

"What does that mean, make it to the top? I'ing in no position to promote you."

She grabs his cheeks and squeezes them together. "I know you not. But you can talk to Charlie. I know she'll listen to you."

"What position do you want?"

"Your wife's."

"My wife's? Gia, now you done lost it for real."

"No, you're going to lose it if you don't play your part in this."

"What you mean? I'm gon' lose what?" He's getting more irritated.

"You know what, don't worry about it. I'll just take your job. How about that?"

"Gia, you're buggin'," he tells her.

She sees he's feeling uneasy about what she just said so she seduces him all over again. He falls for the bait, and when he cums three times over:

"Gia, I'ma see what I can do," he tells her, wiping his dick off with baby wipes.

Gia heads out the door.

The power of the P-U-S-S-Y. She wears a smile on her face as she walks up the hall.

Day 15

Gia walks in Sherry's office. "Hi, you. I came to bring peace. I'm sorry about yesterday. That just happened."

"Gia, please leave my office. If you want to speak with me, please make an appointment."

Gia inspects her face, thinking she's got to be kidding. "Are you that mad about a piece of dick? Girl, I used to know him. We been fuckin' for years. He's a man hoe. Why would you want to be with someone like that anyway? Sherry, you're selling yourself short."

"I'm not selling myself any kind of way. To me, you're the man hoe and he's a jerk off. I don't care what you two do, as long as he takes care of our child. I'm a grown woman. I can take care of myself. Gia, I don't befriend people then shit on'em like you just did."

"Ok, I get it. I'm sorry. I see we come from two different worlds, this is clear. I see that now. So I'll leave you be. However, I want you to know I mean what I said. You deserve more than tricky Ricky."

Gia makes her last remarks as she leaves the office.

"These sensitive bitches. They need to come to my class of the hard knock life."

Gia goes to Ted's office, walking in without asking. "You son of a bitch! You did me wrong you knew I wanted more than admin of the fucking upper offices!"

"Gia, I couldn't just make you operations manager. What you think this is?" he spits. "And lower your voice. Someone may hear you."

Like Gia cares. Putting both hands on the front of his desk, she leans towards him. "You do know I recorded our session that day when I cuffed you."

His eyes grow huge. "Gia, are you blackmailing me?"

"What do you think? You know what, ask Janise sense you boning her too."

"Who told you that lie? Janise and I have never—"

She cuts him off, reaching across his desk giving him a soft smack on his face. "I know you put that little thing you call a dick in'a. That's why you moved her up over me. She only has a high school diploma. I have my masters. Now you fix this, or that tape goes viral."

"Viral? As in the internet viral?"

"You got it. Now you get me operations. I worked hard for it. I don't fuck with white men … well for the money I do. But that's here nor there. Just get me the damn position," she notes as she vanishes, leaving him sitting behind his desk worried about the repercussions if that tape leaks.

***

Bill calls Gia into his office.

"Yes you called me, Bill?"

"Yes, I did. Take a seat, please."

"Are you going to introduce me to the lady?" Gia asks, watching the older lady that's standing by his chair.

"This is Charlie Burt's mother."

"Hi, Gia. My name is Mrs. Burt. You can call me Seria."

"Hi, Seria. Nice to meet you," Gia says, taking a seat in front of his desk.

"Gia, I guess you're wondering what I brought you in here for?"

"Kinda," she voices, not taking her eyes off Seria.

"I brought you in to talk about the Error in the Hold accounts. Ted and I spoke about this. We came up with creating a new department, calling it Error in the Hold accounts. This department will consist of 20 employees and one operations manager. It will have a million-dollar budget for payroll the first year. The operational manager will be offered a salary of $200,000 the first year, receiving a commission bonus at the end of each year. The office will be on the 4th floor of this building. I have computers up there. We were going to do this a while ago but it kinda got put on

the back burner. So I am offering this project to you. Ted informed me you did such a good job when you were helping him out. He added you have an eye for errors. Is this something you would like to do?" he asks.

Gia can't contain her excitement. "Yes, yes. I'll take it all, thanks." She smiles ear to ear.

"Good. For the time being, we're pulling you from your duty as admin. You'll move upstairs and start going through files manually. I'll send you five people to help you until we can get the computer programmers up there. The phones are on already. You'll interview the staff that may apply for the position. Let me know what date you would like for us to list the positions."

"Thanks so much. I won't let you down."

"No, don't let Ted down. He's the one that convinced me to do this. And Gia, please no more blackmails. It's not a good look for you."

Gia's smile quickly dissolves. She can't believe he said that in front of Mrs. Burt.

"You're dismissed," he tells her coldly.

Mrs. Burt follows her out the office. "Gia, Gia," she calls in a low voice.

Gia makes an about face.

"Can we meet for lunch?" she asks her.

"Sure. You wanna meet me after you heard that?"

"Chile, who cares about that? We women do what it takes. What woman you know that's on top hasn't slept their way there? My husband owned this piece of shit and many a women slept with him to make it to the top. So I'll meet you at Tony and Joes at 8 p.m. tomorrow, if you know where that is."

"Sounds good to me," Gia lets out.

"Good." Mrs. Burt's smile sticks to her face as she walks away.

Day 16

"I wonder what she wants to see me about," Gia says as she sits at her kitchen table eating bacon, eggs and drinking her morning coffee.

Three hours later Gia walks in the office. People are gathered around.

"Gia, did you hear what happened?" Cathy asks.

"No, what happened?" she asks Cathy, Bill's clerk.

"It's Sherry. She got into a car accident. Her brakes went out. She hit a truck head on."

"OMG!" Gia lets out, holding her mouth. "Tell me she's alright?"

"Yes, thank God. But her child is dead. Her and Mr. Thompson's child is dead."

"Her what? My God, where is she?" Gia says.

"At home. She's taking the week off. He is too."

"Shouldn't she take more than that? I mean both of them?"

"Yeah, but she said she wants to get back to work soon. It's for the best, she said. He has too much work to do, he told Bill." Cathy relies the gossip.

"I'll send her flowers. What's her address?" Gia asks with a nice cheese on her face.

"Hold on, let me look." Cathy looks in her computer. She prints it out then hands it to Gia. "Would you rather I do it for you, Gia?"

"No, I'll take care of it."

Gia leaves the second floor, taking the stairway.

"I killed her child. Forgive me, Lord. I didn't mean for her child to die. I bled the brakes thinking she would be in the car alone. But she wasn't, that's my fault. I'm sorry, Lord, I am. I would never kill a child. I will make it up to her, I promise," she continues to express, crying real tears.

She feels so guilty. For once in her life she feels pain in her heart for someone else.

Not being able to get nothing done today, she turns out the lights to her new plush office, making her way to meet Mrs. Burt.

"Goodnight you all, thanks for working overtime. I greatly appreciate it," she tells the four staff members that stayed so they can make overtime monies.

She gets in her car, drives to Georgetown parks, makes her way into Tony and Joe's restaurant.

"Hello, I'm looking for a Mrs. Burt," she tells the hostess at the front door.

The hostess reads over her roster. "I found her. Follow me," she orders.

Gia follows her.

"Here you are, the VIP room. Would you like something to drink while you wait for your waiter?" she offers.

"Yes, a tall glass of red wine. Any kind," Gia tells her, kinda wondering why it's another lady with Mrs. Burt.

"Hi, Gia," Seria greets happily.

"Hi." Gia smiles

Charlie rises out her chair in slow motion. Tears fill her eyes. "It is you. Gia, my Gia."

"What, lady? Who are you?" Gia raises concern.

Seria stands beside Gia. "Gia, this is your mother. My daughter, Charlie."

Gia stares at the both of them back and forth. "My what?"

"Gia, will you please give us a minute of your time so I can explain this all to you. I know this sounds crazy but I think after you hear us out you will understand," Charlie speaks up.

Gia hesitates, thinking she is one of the company head bosses so she sits.

Charlie sits across from her so she can get a good look at her long lost child.

"Gia?" Seria calls. "I have some pictures here." She pulls them out her TOD's purse. "Gia, this is your two sisters, Sandy and Xian. I raised Xian until she was 16 years old. She fell ill of a rare blood disease. She died. I make it a point to visit her grave every day, making sure she has fresh flowers. Charlie comes down every six months. We celebrate her birthday every year together. Sandy ... we don't know who adopted her. We thought you two were being raised together. We found out that wasn't so, that Sandy moved to another home. Her parents said they couldn't handle her anymore. We searched and searched for the both of you, coming up with nothing. Both adoptions were what they call *closed* adoptions.

"When you all were born, Charlie was 14. My husband, her father, threatened to disown her from the family, meaning she would've been put out with nowhere to go and no money. So I sent her to my sister's house and told him she gave you all up but I kept one of you. He said that was ok after he got used to her. My friend took you two so we could see you all, but when her husband left her she sold you two without telling me. Old bitch, I hate her to this day for it. Well the lady she sold you to put you two up for adoption when she went broke. That is how we lost the two of you. Believe me when I say I wish things could have been different."

Gia is so shocked but happy her parents are happy to see her. Now she understands why Bill was standoffish. *Makes sense now.*

Gia lifts out her seat, runs around the table hugging her mother for the first time. She's so happy to meet her. She knows now she'll be loved by the woman she thought didn't love or want her. It feels good to know she was wanted.

Day 17

Gia called her sister Sandy. She didn't want her mother and grandmother to know she talked to her 'cause she wasn't sure if Sandy wanted to be in their life. She tells Sandy everything they told her. Sandy said she didn't want to meet them. She didn't ever want them to know she was alive. She told Gia she just wanted to keep playing the twin game at the company. No one notices when she is Sandy or Gia. She likes that. She hates Charlie even more now for not picking her over the other twin to take care of. For letting them go over money. This she lets Gia know.

Gia was sad for her but she told her she respects that. She'll do anything for her sister. She feels she has to. She was born one hour older than Sandy, plus Sandy had it hard with her adopted family being beaten all the time. At least that's what she told Gia.

Sandy sits on the sofa in Gia's living room watching TV.

"Gia, why you still living in here we making all this money?"

"I'on know. I think I'm attached to it. I've been in here for so long. Plus I like apartment living. All that big house stuff is you. Not me," she explains.

"Oh well. I think we need a new place," Sandy says.

"Whatever you say. Why don't you go and get a new place? We spilt the money 50-50 anyways."

"You right. I'll think about it. My apartment is falling apart anyway. But this is what I came to tell you. I got this gig. Merry said he thinks we can make at least two million off it each."

"Oh yeah? What kind of gig is it?" Gia asks while cooking dinner for them.

"We gon' rob this bank. He know the lady that runs it. She gon' turn off the cameras while we rob the joint. She told him four million would be in the vault. We'll just go in, get the money, split it three ways. Sounds easy, right?"

"Yap. When he gonna do it?" Gia questions.

"Tomorrow at 6 a.m. when the bank lady is opening up," she informs.

"Let's do it. But this is the last scam for me. I just wanna get to know my family and be loved. I wanna be square."

"Fine then," Sandy says, frowning up her face at Gia.

Gia brings the food to the table. "I may have to leave you here. I gotta meet Mrs. Burt. We're going to the movies."

"Gia, we always eat dinner together since we been back together. What's going on with you? This family shit is getting to your head."

"No it's not. I just wanna get to know them like I get to know you. What's wrong with that? They're not taking me from you at all. It's not like that," Gia tries to explain.

"Gia, when you start liking the movies? We always watch them in the house."

"I know but tonight I'm watching a movie with my grandmother. Now eat up."

Sandy looks at her food. "I'm not hungry," she pouts, walking out the front door.

Day 18

It's 5:30 a.m. Gia, Merry, and Sandy sit outside the SunTrust Bank. The lady drives up. They all approach her wearing black masks. She acts shocked. Hurrying, she opens the door to the bank taking them to the vault. They hurry, collecting all the money they can fit into the gray bags.

"Ok, I'll pick mines up at your house, Mary," the lady that runs the back says.

"No you won't."

Bloc! Bloc!

Two shots ring out.

"Why you kill'em both?"

"'Cause two is bedda than four. Now let's go before people start coming in."

They ride back to the apartment.

"What we gon' do wit' all this money?" one of them speaks out.

"Spend it, what else? Four million—two for you, two for me," one of them says.

They laugh. They start running around the apartment, throwing money in the air.

"We're rich for real!" they yell.

"Ok look, I'ma see you tomorrow. Don't be spending all this money around here. Keep your job for a while, then after shit dies down you can start spending. Buy nice stuff, you get it?"

"I do, don't worry."

"I can't believe you shot her."

Day 19

"Hello, Gia," Sherry says as she enters Gia's office.

"Hello," she speaks back. "Sorry about your child again," Gia sincerely tells her for the fifth time.

"I know you are. Just checking on you. Sorry about that day I got upset with you. I know I told you but I'm sorry."

"It's ok. Look, Sherry, I have so much to do. Can we talk lata?"

"Oh, ok. Are you going to hire me up here with you?" Sherry asks.

Gia looks at her. "No, I got enough people working here already."

"Oh. Oh, but I thought that night you came to see me and we … you know, had fun. You and me …" Sherry is confused.

Looking at Sherry, "That was to make you feel bedda. Sherry, you too weak to be my woman. Now I told you I got shit to do," she says, putting her head down, reading her papers.

Sherry eyes start to water. She leaves Gia's office in a rage. She stops at Bill's office.

"Mr. Smith, you have one minute."

He sees it's her. "Sure, come in."

"Thanks. It's about Gia. I think she killed all your employees. I think she tried to kill me that day, not knowing my child would be in the car."

Bill tells her to keep it to herself. He tells her to let him take care of it, thanking her again. Before she exits his office, "Did you tell anyone else this story?"

"No, but I didn't want you to be next, you know. So I thought I would tell you first."

"Thanks again. I'll handle it. And be looking for something extra on your paycheck for being brave enough to come by and tell me."

"You welcome," she tells him, walking out his office snickering.

He calls his ex-wife to his office, telling her what Sherry told him.

"We'll handle it. Call her to the office," Charlie demands.

He calls Gia to his office.

She walks in. "You call me?"

"Yes baby girl we did." He tells her what Sherry told them.

"You want me to handle it, dad?" she asks. He's not used to being called dad but he likes it.

Charlie looks at him, waiting for an answer. "What?! That would be a murder and we would be in on it," he tells her.

"Bill, I just got her back. I'm not losing her to prison. No, not happening. So either you have her killed or you let her do what she's been doing to make it to the top."

"How did you know it was me?" Gia asks.

"I put two and two together when you blackmailed Ted," Bill assures her. He's not stupid.

"Oh."

"Ok, just do what you do and be careful—in which I'm sure you will."

Day 20

"Gia, here are the names for the party." Bill's new assistant hands them to her.

"OK. I'll take care of them," she says, walking to her office.

"Hi, Gia," Janise Says with glee walking past her in the hall.

"Hi, Janise," she speaks back. She's wondering why she's speaking to her. Only if she knew she had her man for dinner last night.

She makes it to her office.

"Good morning, Mrs. Shirley. The designer of the new mansion you're buying called. He said call him. He needs to go over some things about the plans with you. Mr. Tattaes called as well about your new Lexus coupe. He said to call him immediately, something about the insurance number. He left off the last digit. And do you want me to send Ms.

Sherry Wong's family some flowers?" Cathy, Bill's old assistant, asks.

Gia kept her promise and took her with her. She's paying her more money. She stops in her tracks. "Mrs. Wong? What happened to her?" Gia asks.

"She died in the garage around 4 o'clock yesterday after work."

"Wait. What did they say happened to her?"

"The police don't know. All they saying is she dropped dead. They won't know until the autopsy."

"Man, that's crazy."

"That's what I said."

"Send them some flowers, by all means," she orders Cathy.

She walks in her office, closes the door laughing. "Got yo ass. So that's why Janise so happy today. That's why she spoke to me. She thinks her competition is dead. Little do she know. Life's not bad here. I could quit this job but it feels good to be at the top, looking down on muthafuckas for a change. I think I'll stay right here. And see what's in store for me. Maybe I'll become the owner one day. Soon ... really soon."

Day 21

She leaves her job after a hard day's work. She drives to the Catholic church not too far from where her office is. Parking, she gets out. Walking in Gia stands in line to see the priest to give her confession. She's the last person for today. Taking her seat in the booth, she starts confessing her sins.

"Forgive me, Father, for I have sinned."

"What have you done, my child?"

"For the last 21 days I've been killing people. I injected poison into a stranger's neck. She's dead. I poisoned a lady on my job, then I smothered her. She died too. I was partly the reason for a child's death that I will regret for the rest of my life. I also gave her mother some killer mushrooms in her pepper steak. She died. Then I killed a bank teller. Oh, I lied on my application to get my job. I said I went to Harvard so they would hire me for this job. I also blackmailed a man."

The priest is silent, also shocked. He doesn't know what to do. *I can't call the police and report this*, are his thoughts as he sits on the other side of the makeshift confession booth. The real one is under construction so they had to make a temporary one.

"Is there anything else?" he asks.

She quickly walks out her side of the booth into his. Raising the long knife, "It's one more thing. I killed my sista at a bank robbery! I'm Sandy!"

ON SALE NOW!

JORDAN BELCHER PRESENTS
REVENGE
IS BEST SERVED
COLD
J.J. JACKSON